DETROIT PUBLIC LIBRARY

Brows..g Library

DATE DUE

JAN 29 1994
FEB 18 1994
MAR 12 1994
MAR 26 1994
DEC 16 1995
JUL 18 1998
MAR 03 2000

DEC 22 1998

THE ALTERNATIVE DETECTIVE

Tor books by Robert Sheckley

The Alternative Detective
Immortality, Inc.

THE ALTERNATIVE DETECTIVE

ROBERT SHECKLEY

A TOM DOHERTY ASSOCIATES BOOK
NEW YORK

c.2
M

This is a work of fiction. All the characters and events portrayed in this book are fictitious, and any resemblance to real people or events is purely coincidental.

THE ALTERNATIVE DETECTIVE

Copyright © 1993 by Robert Sheckley

All rights reserved, including the right to reproduce this book, or portions thereof, in any form.

This book is printed on acid-free paper.

A Forge Book
Published by Tom Doherty Associates, Inc.
175 Fifth Avenue
New York, N.Y. 10010

Edited by David G. Hartwell

Library of Congress Cataloging-in-Publication Data

Sheckley, Robert.
The alternative detective / Robert Sheckley.
p. cm.
"A Tom Doherty Associates book."
ISBN 0-312-85023-9 (hardcover)
1. Private investigators—United States—Fiction.
I. Title.
PS3569.H392A79 1993
813'.54--dc20 93-11520
CIP

BL
DEC 22 1993

First edition: October 1993

Printed in the United States of America

0 9 8 7 6 5 4 3 2 1

To Gail, with all my love.

THE ALTERNATIVE DETECTIVE

FRANKIE FALCONE 1

THERE WAS A light tap on the door. I didn't get excited. Occasionally someone mistakes my office for the back entrance to the dentist down the hall.

"Come in," I called.

In walked a short, heavyset young guy dressed in a Hawaiian shirt, tweed sports jacket, Levis, and a wide leather belt with a brass buckle the size of a small serving plate that said REMINGTON FIREARMS. He had black hair, brown eyes, and his skin was deeply tanned.

"Is this the Alternative Detective Agency?" he asked, like he didn't quite believe it despite the cracked gold lettering on the door.

I admit the setup doesn't look like much. A mean little office in a row of mean offices in a two-story office building that must have been old when Peter Stuyvesant was still stumping around Manhattan. A bookcase with the 1976 *Britannica* in it, *Volume 5, CASTER to COLE* missing. Scarred oak desk. Window behind the desk with a view of the crumbling storefronts on State Street. No carpet, but a permanent gray stain on the once-varnished floor where some sort of floor covering had lain, probably back a hundred years ago when Snuff's Landing had been a prosperous Hudson River port. On the wall, a few bad imitations of Dutch masters that Mylar had put up during her brief enthusiasm for me and the agency. Back when she'd been planning to help me, had even considered becoming a detective herself. We'd had some dreams back then, before Sheldon came on the scene.

"I know it doesn't look like much," I told the kid. "That's lucky for you; you got in just before the big expansion, while we're still operating at the same old rates."

That didn't impress him, or even strike him as funny. He sat back in my client chair, which is made mostly of scuffed varnish and peeled imitation leather. He said after a while, "I guess Sam Spade's office looked a little like this. But he had a secretary."

"You been watching too many TV detectives," I told him. "Now, what can I do for you, sir?"

"I guess you don't remember me, Mr. Draconian," he said. "I'm Frankie Falcone, your nephew."

He was my sister Rita's oldest boy. Rita lives in Oregon, so I don't see too much of her. Must have been six, seven years since I'd seen Frankie. This was the first time Rita had sent me a customer, if that's what he was.

"Take a seat, Frankie. How's Rita?"

"She's fine. She sent me this picture to give you." He pulled it out of a knapsack he was carrying.

It showed a big frame house with a long shady porch. There was an old refrigerator on one side of the porch, a glider-type couch on the other. There was a wrecked truck off to one side and big trees behind. Standing on the porch from right to left there was Rita, there were Arlene and Doris, the fat twins. There was Frankie, shorter than Rita, and there was a sweet-faced girl with short fluffy blonde hair standing beside him. They had their arms around each other's waists.

"Who's this?" I asked.

"That's Trish Johnson," Frankie said. "We got married last year."

"And these guys?"

The two dark, moustached young men, one tall and thin and serious looking, the other short and barrel chested with a scar on his cheek that could have been put there by a knife, turned out to be Antonio and Carlos Ordoñez, Mexican craftsmen who worked for Frankie during sailboarding season. The house backed onto woods and mountains. On the back porch, leaning against the clapboard wall, were two tall conical objects painted in bright colors like psychedelic sarcophagi.

"What are those?" I asked.

"Couple of my sailboards," Frankie said. "That's what I do."

"Sail sailboards?"

"Yes, and I also design and build them. Falcone Double X competition boards, that's what they're called."

So this chubby and bucolic youth was a designer, manufacturer and entrepreneur. I looked at him with new respect.

I put the photo in a desk drawer. "So what's the problem?" I asked.

Frankie took a seat and told me about it.

After he graduated from high school, Frankie did a lot of odd jobs. For a while he pumped gas and fixed cars down at the local Flying A. Worked for a while as a driver for Weyerhauser until they closed the Hood River operation. Then he took a job working for Virgil Sibbs, who made fiberglass fishing boats. Virgil went bankrupt and packed up one day and went away. People had suspected he wasn't much good anyhow.

Frankie started doing wood and fiberglass work, because he had more or less inherited Sibbs' machinery. When sailboards began to get popular, he was right there at the start. He liked sailboarding and he was good at it. He started to build boards. Trish helped him study board and sail design. He turned out to have a feel for what one of those little hulls would do under a variety of sea and wind conditions. He had a sculptor's touch with the polyurethane. Pretty soon a Falcone XX became known as a pretty hot board. People didn't know the XX stood for Dos Equis, Frankie's favorite beer.

Sailboarding became very big in the town of Hood River in Oregon's Columbia Gorge. Sailboarding schools opened up, the beaches began to fill, first on weekends, then all week long, all summer long. Sailboarding was in, and the Columbia Gorge was one of the best places in the world to do it. True, you didn't get the surf like on Maui. But a faithful and reliable wind howled down the Gorge most days, twenty, thirty knots or better. The waters were too tight to build up much wave action. This was a great place to learn speed and maneuverability in broken-water conditions.

Sailboard making is a highly competitive occupation. Frankie thought he'd made the breakthrough when Industrias Marisol, a Spanish company, ordered two of his boards, then another two. It was good publicity. Frankie started to hear about guys taking firsts and seconds on his Falcone XX boards at Lake Geneva and Palma de Mallorca.

Then Industrias Marisol asked him for five custom boards, specially rigged, and they wanted them in a hurry. They promised to pay as soon as the boards arrived.

"So I shipped five of my competition boards to Industrias Marisol, this place in Ibiza, Spain. They got my full assortment. A short board, a slalom, a speed board, a wave board and one transition. Everything fully equipped. Masts, booms, universals, sails, board bags. They'd bought my boards before, so I trusted them. They needed the boards quick for a European tour and offered me a third above what I usually get. I got the order together and shipped them out. The agent from Industrias Marisol called me from Spain and said his check would be in the mail next day. I get a notice from my shipping company that the boards have arrived and cleared customs. Two weeks go by. No check. I telephone Industrias Marisol but there's no answer. I send a telegram. Nothing. I don't know who's got my boards or my money. More than ten thousand dollars' value in that shipment."

"What do you think I can do for you, Frankie?"

"Get back my money for me. Mom said you've got contacts over there."

I thought about it. Theoretically, Frankie had an open and shut case. Assuming the paperwork was in order, he could lodge a claim in a Spanish court for recovery. Spanish justice is sometimes slow, but it works pretty good.

But maybe it wouldn't have to go that far. Maybe just having somebody talk to the Marisol guy would clear things up. Nobody wants the law called in. Maybe someone just needs to tell him, give the guy back his boards or send him his money. Most people are honest but absentminded. And I wouldn't even have to do it myself. I had Harry Hamm working for me on Ibiza.

"I can't make any promises," I said, "but we do have one of our operatives in Ibiza and I'll see what I can do for you. I'll need a retainer before I begin."

"How much of one?"

"A couple hundred would be a good beginning."

"How about a hundred and we'll make a bad beginning?"

I accepted. It would barely cover our telephone and cable costs, but what the hell, I'd needed a case to give to Harry. If I didn't keep him working, I was going to lose my operative. And then my whole scheme would fall apart.

I wrote down the pertinent information from Frankie. He was going to Philadelphia that evening for the convention, back to Oregon two days later. I told him I'd be in touch and to give Rita my love.

After Frankie left, I thought long and hard. Was this the long-awaited sign? Was it time for me to shed America and its strange ways and return to my Europe of sweet memory? Ibiza—it had to be! And yet, it didn't seem possible. Frankie's case wouldn't pay much; not even my airfare to Spain. Reluctantly, I decided against going myself. This case must be one for the other operative of the Alternative Detective Agency.

I rolled a sheet of paper in the typewriter and typed out a letter of instructions to Harry Hamm, my man in Ibiza. But I thought to myself, it's coming; my day is coming.

MOTHER 2

Mom lives in Florida and she loves my being a private detective.

"Who did you kill recently?" she cackles when I come to the Golden Shores Retirement Center for my semiannual visit.

She introduces me to her friends, "Hey, Sadie, meet my son Hobart, the private detective." Sadie, skinny little stick in a pale yellow spotted dress, looks me up and down.

"Hey, Mom, you know I don't kill people," I remind her.

"Then who'd you shake down recently?" she asks, and bursts into gales of laughter. My mom is, like they say, uninhibited. It's something my father always held against her. And when I visit him at his retirement home—the Southern Breezes Trailer Court in Key Largo, Florida—he always asks after her with a supercilious air.

"Your mother, the loudmouth—how is she?" he asks.

"Pick up a telephone and find out," I tell him. "She's only a couple hundred miles away, straight up A1A."

"You don't have to tell me where she is; didn't I put her there myself?"

"Well, why don't you ever get in touch?"

"Listen, *boychik,*" he says to me in his fake Yiddish accent, "I had to live with that woman for twenty-seven years, the first eighteen or so raising you, and the rest taking care of her swollen ankles until the good Lord blessed me with the idea of a retirement home."

Actually, it hadn't gone that way at all. It was Mom who had finally left him, declaring that twenty-seven years of his acid wit and general air of know-it-all unpleasantness was quite enough, thank you very much. Especially since they had been unable to agree on where to retire. Mom liked Golden Shores because she had a couple of friends there, like Mrs. Salazarri who used to run the deli in Asterion, New Jersey, where we had lived for a lot of those years; she'd decided to retire after her husband Pep' was killed by a teenage stickup kid from Irvington. And Golden Shores was not far from the North Miami Elder Citizens' Center, with its Ukrainian folk dances on Tuesday nights and its bridge raffles, ping-pong ball guessing contests and other forms of hirth and milarity.

"Me call her?" Pop asked. "You must be crazy! Start talking to that woman and I might end up hooked again."

Pop talked in fishing analogies. He had come down to Key Largo for the—you guessed it—fishing. Bonefish, marlin, yellow-tail. He was a tall, skinny, old guy with a very tan face and a big grin. Always a couple days' worth of white stubble on his face. He'd been shaving every day during his working life as a tailor and furrier, and he figured that was enough.

Nice parents, but they weren't much help to me when I came back to America after nearly twenty years living abroad. Not their fault. Nobody could have helped. My first company was Alternative Services Corporation. I set it up after returning to the States in 1979 after the Istanbul disaster. I didn't know what to do with myself back in America.

It hurts to be Johnny Greenhorn in your own country. Almost from a sense of self-protection, I decided to form up the A.S.C.

I'm one of those people who lived in Europe in the sixties and seventies. In Europe, among other things, I had been a clothing and junk jewelry wholesaler, selling to hippies mainly. Now, I used my contacts with hippie organizations and individuals all over Europe to become a supplier of craftsmen's and farmers' tools and implements to communes and New Age groups all over western Europe. I was the founder and proprietor of The Alternative Services Corporation.

I was the man to contact if you were really in a rush for a waterless toilet for your campground in the Sierra Nevadas, an Aladdin kerosene lamp for your electricityless finca in Ibiza, a wheel seeder with cultivating attachments for your subsistence garden near Aix-en-Provence, a Shaker furniture kit for the eternal homespun look, or even a small foundry for the primitivists in western Wales. I had the answers to those and quite a few other questions. I charged ten percent over the manufacturer's list price and you paid postage, but I got the goods for you. I did the calling and harassed the manufacturers until they got off their asses and got the goods out of the warehouse and onto a plane to you. With some frequently used items, like tie-dye chemicals, I maintained a modest stock in a warehouse behind the Flying A station in West New York, next town up from Snuff's Landing.

I also served as a communication network for many of these people, and I was called upon from time to time to locate someone who might have used my service and had gone missing. People don't go to the straight police so much in the whole-earth community. They don't go to private detectives, either, but I was one of the avatars of the new breed.

And I ran all this from Snuff's Landing, New Jersey. Not a bad life, you say. Yes, but have you considered the size of my support payments? I was in Snuff's Landing because I had inherited the house on Elm Street from my Uncle Marv. I had moved in there with my most recent wife, Mylar. Now I was waiting for Mylar to complete the last stages of the slow, almost stately dissolution of our marriage and move away; go back to Louisiana, maybe, with her suitcases of Vedantic philosophy books she never got around to reading, and her clippings from her two years' modelling in Paris, or wherever she pleased, taking her curly auburn hair, sweet smile and long days of sulky silence somewhere else, so I could sell Uncle Marv's house and go live in some place with a little class.

But Mylar didn't go, not even when Sheldon declared his love for her. And I didn't dare leave the house for fear it would somehow be sold out from under me. And anyhow, I wasn't thinking straight. Back from Europe, I was in limbo, numbed out, culture shocked from returning to an America I didn't understand or sympathize with after nearly twenty years in Europe. People were talking about things I'd never heard of. I'd missed two decades of television. I felt out of it, a foreigner even though with my speech I could pass as a native.

I didn't know that was the trouble then, of course. If you had asked me, I might not even have known that I was miserably unhappy. I was too depressed even for ironic contemplation of my own depression. I had descended into the sorry game of repeating to myself bits of sophomoric moral philosophy, in an attempt to head off the utter collapse that had opened beneath my feet when I found that my life made no sense at all.

Grimly I chewed on uplifting aphorisms: Life is beautiful anywhere, I told myself as I walked along the low, marshy, smelly New Jersey foreshore, with its stunted trees and sooty birds and sour little towns. And I steeled myself to face the truth: that life isn't very good but it's all you've got. And all the time, though I didn't know it, the changes were stirring.

DAMASCENE 3

THE WOMAN KNOWN as Damascene came to me the very next day in Snuff's Landing, New Jersey.

Snuff's Landing is one of the decaying Hudson River towns that line the shabby foreshore between Hoboken and Fort Lee.

As usual, I was in my dingy office on Sisal Street and I remember that I had just reached page 666 in Motley's *Rise and Fall of the Dutch Republic,* which is exactly the sort of book to read when you have a business like mine with long gaps between the exciting bits, if any. Then my first customer of the year, aside from Frankie, tapped lightly on the door and came in.

This was very welcome since it was already June.

She was a tall, willowy girl with sunstreaked blonde hair. Her mouth looked sort of trembly and vulnerable. Her eyes were dark and gray, and she had peculiar little lights in the irises. She was wearing a severely tailored dark suit which did not hide her shape; it was that happy simultaneity of ampleness and slenderness that some fortunate women possess.

"Are you Hobart Draconian?" she asked.

"Just like the sign on the door says," I told her. "Who are you?"

"Men call me Damascene," she said. "I come from Montclair, New Jersey, where the pomegranates grow." She smiled at me and a lock of hair fell fetchingly over one eye, giving her that Veronica Lake look that I find so hard to resist.

"Unusual name," I commented, sizing up her good legs as she sat in the client's chair facing my desk.

"It's not my real name," she said. "I was just kidding about that. It's something I do when I get nervous. Actually, I'm Rachel Starr with two *r*'s and the first thing I have to ask you is if the name Vedra means anything to you."

Vedra is an uninhabited island off the coast of Ibiza. Ibiza is one of the four Balearic islands that lie in the western Mediterranean between Spain and France. Vedra was the place we used to go for sunset watching, back a million years ago when I lived on Ibiza with Kate and we did things like that.

"What do you know about Vedra?" I asked.

"I know that you and Alex shared a house near there one summer."

"Alex? You mean Alex Sinclair?"

She nodded.

I'd lost track of Alex years ago. He and I had been pretty tight for a while.

"What's the problem?" I asked.

"Alex said if anything ever happened to him, I should look you up."

"So what's happened?"

"He's missing."

I nodded. It would have to be something like that. That's why they come to me.

"Where was he last seen?" I asked her.

"Paris."

I straightened up in my chair. "What was he doing?"

"He was playing in a rock band. Five-string electric banjo, I believe. He left Amsterdam to rejoin his group."

"Just a minute." I swung my feet off the desk and found a pad and a Bic. "What was the name of his group?"

"Les Monstres Sacrés."

"That sounds like Alex's sort of group all right. Please continue."

"I know he arrived in Paris. He sent me a telegram from De

Gaulle Airport. He was going to telephone me when he had a hotel room."

"Obviously he didn't."

"No, he did not. I didn't hear anything from him. That was three weeks ago."

"I don't mean to be harsh," I said, "but is it possible maybe he was ducking you?"

"I don't think so," Rachel said. "He'd given me his power of attorney to clear out his bank accounts and sell some property. I'm holding nearly eighty thousand dollars in Alex's money. That, my friend, is not chicken liver."

"I agree he probably wasn't trying to duck you," I said. "Did you have anyone to call and ask about him? A mutual friend?"

She shook her head. "Alex was very specific about that. If anything happened, I wasn't to try anyone but you."

"You've come to the right place," I told her. "The right man, I mean. This is definitely my kind of case."

Rachel didn't look convinced. She looked at me, doubt clouding over her large gray eyes.

"What kind of a gun do you carry?" she asked.

"I don't carry a gun. I believe in an American citizen's inalienable right to not bear arms. As a matter of fact, I'm a member of the Anti-Rifle Association of America."

She looked me over, sizing me up. "But you're tough, right? Karate, stuff like that?"

I shook my head. "Violent movements put my back out. And my doctor has warned me to avoid getting hit on the head."

"But what do you do in a dangerous situation?"

"I perform the instantaneous intuitive leap that tells me how to handle the situation."

"You mean that you fake it?"

I nodded. "Faking it. A term used by Paul Simon, one of my favorite philosophers. Yes, that's what I do."

"I'm not really convinced," Rachel said. "Can you give me one reason why anyone would hire you rather than the first name she comes across in the Yellow Pages?"

I shrugged and gave her my half smile. "Because I can cut it, lady." A line from *Hud,* one of my favorite movies. "But there are several more compelling reasons. You have noticed no doubt that I don't wear a suit. Private detectives who wear suits charge at least twenty-five percent more than private detectives who wear Levis."

She still looked doubtful. "Are you at least tough? A body-builder, maybe, beneath your apparent scrawniness? A knife thrower?"

I had to smile. She had been taken in by appearances, as so many are. Spiritually I am a tall, lean, cool dude with long hair in a headband. But in physical aspect you might not know that, since I am shorter than average and inclined toward a very slight dumpiness.

"I try to avoid violence," I told her. "Look, Rachel, I'm the right person to find Alex. Do you think you can hire a man with short hair and a three-piece suit to hang out in the Barrio Chino in Barcelona and come up with leads? Or rap with the Senegalese dope dealers in Les Halles? Or trade hits with the jokers in the Milky Way in Amsterdam?"

"And you can get into those places?"

"Lady, those places are my home," I told her.

"I don't have a great deal of money," she told me.

"It doesn't take much to get me going. My air fares, meagre expenses, and a hundred dollars a day pin money. That means I don't earn a thing and have to sleep in youth hostels. But what the hell, it's for Alex."

"All right," she said, "you're a little weird, but Alex said to trust you. Maybe we can afford a better class of hotel than youth hostels."

"We?"

"I'm going with you."

"Why?"

"To make sure you don't run away with my money. And to find Alex. And because I've never been to Europe before."

Well, what the hell. She was a foxy lady. And I was going back to Europe.

HARRY HAMM 4

I sent Frankie Falcone's information on to our man in Ibiza, Harry Hamm. Harry is an ex-cop who spent twenty-eight years on the Jersey City force. That was back when Madge was still alive and the twins, Dorrie and Florence, were living at home in the two-story frame house on Kearney Street. Harry's retired now and living on the island of Ibiza. He owns a small finca, where he raises two varieties of almond trees and can talk in dialect with his Ibicenco neighbors.

Although he's officially retired and has a small income from his pension, he's not opposed to taking on a job from time to time. People have a way of bringing him work. Unofficially, of course: the Spanish police don't license foreign detectives to operate in their territory.

But there are some things the police on Ibiza can't or don't want to handle: rip-offs between rival narcotics gangs; the theft by one thief of a hundred thousand dollars' worth of Renaissance paintings belonging to another thief and never registered with the Spanish authorities; the recovery of a million dollar ransom paid in a rescue attempt that failed.

Harry didn't know any of this until I pointed it out that day in the Peña in Ibiza when the Alternative Detective Agency really came into existence.

Harry had retired last year and moved to Ibiza. The first time he came to Ibiza was to help his son, who'd been put into the Ibiza lockup during the infamous hippie riots of 1969. Harry had gone there to bail him out. It had taken a little longer than usual, because Harry didn't know which people to give bribes to, and because, in Spain, even the bribes must be laid out with proper form and due gravity. By the time he got it all squared away and got his boy out, Harry had worked up a love for the island. Something about the spine of pine-clad mountains, the warm, tideless sea, the people. That Ibiza magic.

Harry started returning every year. First he came over in summer, during crazy season, but that really wasn't to his taste; he didn't like mixing with hot weather weirdos. He'd started taking his vacations in winter, when Ibiza is at its best. He picked up a little finca there, and, after Madge died and the twins moved to Cleveland, Harry took his retirement and moved to Ibiza.

I'd met him there. It wasn't long before Kate and I were breaking up, and Harry and I used to meet in Manolo's bar in Figueretas to push back the little shot glasses of brandy that were so cheap you could hardly afford not to become an alcoholic. When Harry heard I was starting a detective agency, he thought I was crazy.

"You?" he asked. "A detective agency?"

"Me," I said, rubbing the stringy biceps on my left arm.

"But you don't know a damn thing about it!" Harry said.

"I'll tell you something," I said. "I think there's entirely too much emphasis put on expertise. I read a while ago about this guy who used to get into hospitals posing as a brain surgeon. He did great cases, operations, everything. Then the authorities would catch up with him and he'd go on and find another hospital."

"What the hell has that to do with anything?" Harry said.

"It's obvious what a private detective does. It's even easier than brain surgery. There are books. And there are books which correct the mistakes of the first books. So what's the problem?"

"Licensing, for one."

"I'm not going to set up as a private investigator," I told him.

"I'm going to set up as a research establishment. That's what a detective does, really. Researches people, or situations, in order to uncover evidence to bring certain things to light. There's no license needed to be a freelance researcher."

"Then how'll people know you're really a private detective?"

"Word of mouth," I said.

"It's cockamamie," Harry said.

"If you think that's strange, listen to this: I want you to come into the business with me."

"Me? Get out of here!" Harry said gruffly. But I could see he was pleased. There's nothing like a couple of months of retirement on a fun island, with fun people on all sides of you, to bring on a desire to do almost any damn thing as long as it isn't fun. This is especially true if you're a short, thickset, balding guy with a heavy jaw like Harry, whom you would never mistake for a fun person. Although he was, of course, in his own way, just like all of us.

We went to my apartment in the Peña. Harry came in, took off his hat, tossed it into the wicker chair, draped himself across the couch like a slug wearing madras shorts, lit a cigarette. He looked me up and down like he was appraising me.

"Are you really serious about this?"

"Look at it this way, Harry," I told him. "There's need of a people's detective agency. Not the usual sort of place that caters only to the wealthy, or at least the affluent middle class. No, what about the poor; what about the hippies; haven't they any rights? What about the American exiles living abroad, not really protected by local law, and with nobody they can turn to if something goes wrong?"

"What's wrong with the cops?" Harry asked. "They can't go to them?"

"Nothing's wrong with the cops," I said, "but you know as well as I do, some guy comes to your stationhouse in Jersey City speaking broken English, how much attention is he going to get? He's not even a voter, for chrissakes."

"I guess you got a point there," Harry said.

"This thing can work," I told him.

"All right, let's suppose it can work," Harry said. "I'm the one who knows all about detectives and criminals and cops. What do I need you for? Why don't I set up by myself?"

"Simple, Harry," I said. "If you did that, you'd be lonely. What does the money matter to you? You're retired; you just want something to keep your hand in. Let me be your associate. Your manager. Your boss. Try it, you'll like it."

"You know, Hob," Harry said, "you're like those hippie kids my son was always hanging out with when he lived here."

"What's your son doing now? Still with the longhairs?"

"No. Scott's running a massage parlor in Weehawken."

"At least he's not a hippie," I said.

Harry shook his head impatiently. He had talked enough about his son.

"Well," he said, "it's crazy, but I'll think about it."

That's how I got my man in Ibiza. It was almost as good as being there myself. Almost, but not quite.

IBIZA 5

Ibiza is like you attached Coney Island to Big Sur and put the whole thing under Mexican rule.

Ibiza and its adjacent island of Formentera lie south of Majorca and Minorca, roughly on a line drawn between Valencia and Marseilles.

The island has a reputation as an international spot for jet-setters. It was one of the world centers of the counterculture back in the sixties and seventies. Many people went to Ibiza to live that dream. A lot of them, and their children, are there still. I had been one of those people.

There are a lot of reasons for Ibiza's peculiar charm: the dense interpenetration of different layers of society; the constant arrival and departure of the uncountable thousands who make the island a part-time home. There's prosperity, due in part to Ibiza being one of the favored places to take your ill-gotten gains and live a pleasant life. For a certain type of person, having a good income and living in Ibiza would be two definitions of paradise.

The people come and go. They flow in and out, get into the busses and U-drive-it cars and taxis and fan out over the island. Some have chauffeured cars waiting for them. The ships come in every day from Barcelona and Palma with more tourists, and their cars, Jags and Porsches, that get a lot of wear on their suspensions on the rocky Ibiza roads.

The island is about thirty-five miles long by eight or so wide. Its year-round Spanish population is under fifty thousand. During the summer, over a million people pour in and out.

Ibiza is also one of the important transshipment points on the international heroin and cocaine networks. Not to even bother mentioning marijuana and hashish; let's stick with the big ones. Ibiza is a convenient spot to off-load goods by sea from laboratories in the south of France, Corsica, Italy, and get them aboard other carriers going to northern Europe or North America.

Some of the finest houses in town are owned by dope dealers. They're the elite of the Old City, the crowded, twisting, little, cobblestoned streets of the Peña that runs down to the waterfront. On the ten or so blocks of waterfront there are perhaps a hundred or more bars, restaurants and boutiques crowded together.

Ibiza has a big fashion business. There's a lot of money here. There's a lot of rivalry here if you're into crime. Crime is probably the only interesting occupation on the island. It's the only one people really work at. And kill over.

Ibiza is a great hideaway for all sorts of illegal or semi-illegal people, ranging from ex-concentration camp commandants to topflight art forgers. People tend to congregate here with wealth acquired elsewhere. Other people tend to move in around them, and sometimes succeed in ripping them off. This is a separate layer of crime, distinct from the dope wars.

There are a lot of separate worlds here: ex-Nazis; kept women; homosexuals; almond farmers; police; restaurateurs; dropouts.

There are lots of pretty islands in the Med. What makes Ibiza so special? It's the lifestyle. What is this lifestyle? A mixture of traditional Ibicenco manners and dropout hippie laid-backedness and peace. On Ibiza, not only are there things to enjoy, there's the possibility of learning how to enjoy them. That's important for all sorts of people, including gangsters who want to retire and better themselves.

Ibiza is not one of those places where the natives are invisible. Ibicencos still own most of the property on Ibiza. Some of them are rich. They are a tight society, shrewd, good-humored, passionate, and, above all, tolerant. They are one of history's great generous-minded people. They are peasants. But whoever heard of peasants being interested in outsiders, willing to talk to them, to make friends with them, to marry them, to do anything for them? Go to a village in the Auvergne or the Marche and see how quickly you're accepted. Or go elsewhere in Spain, even to Majorca, the next island. Ibicencos aren't like anyone else. They have handled the tourist invasion well. Ibiza remains Ibiza, not an outpost of England or Canada.

A distinction must be made between Ibicencos and Spaniards. Ibicencos are Spaniards, of course, but they're not like other Spaniards. In fact, it's difficult to isolate a single Spanish type, since Spain is intensely regional and can be divided into at least five distinct regions, with many subdivisions possible. Spaniards are not a homogeneous race; they're a bunch of tribes with a few shared characteristics, living side by side and never quite getting the hang of getting along with each other. Political instability is endemic to Spain, as is violence.

The Ibicencos are part of the Catalan people. But their primary allegiance is not to Catalonia. They are Ibicencos before being Catalans. Ibiza is a distinct and separate civilization. One of the finest the world has produced.

I knew it would be a good idea for me never to go there again.

2

KATE 6

I CALLED MY ex-wife Kate to tell her the news. My daughter Sonya answered. Sonya is fourteen and does real well in school. She lives in Woodstock, New York, and I don't see her or her younger brother, Todd, anywhere near as often as I should. That's because it's difficult for me to see Kate even though we're long divorced and I've married Mylar.

"Hi, kid," I said, "how are you?"

"I'm fine, Daddy," Sonya said. "I got straight A's again on my report card."

We chatted for a few minutes. Then I knew that I had to say it.

"Listen, darling, I don't think I'll be able to come to your graduation week after next."

"Oh, Daddy! What's come up this time?"

"It's a job, honey. Necessary to keep us all eating. I'll be leaving in a day or two."

"And when will you be back?"

"Probably three weeks, a month. I am sorry."

"I know, Daddy. Good luck. Just a moment. Mommy wants to speak to you."

And then Katie's voice, a little anxious. "Hob? What's this about a job?"

"It's a case for the agency. I can't tell you much about it. It'll take a few weeks."

"Will it pay anything?"

"There's a bonus arrangement. It could pay pretty well."

"It would be nice if you could help out with Sonya's orthodontia. I know it's not in the agreement, but I just don't have the money, and she's a pretty kid, Hob; it would be a shame not to straighten out her teeth now, when it's relatively easy."

"Sure, I'll be able to help."

"Thanks. Where are you going?"

"Paris."

"Not Ibiza?"

"Not if I can help it."

"Even going to Paris. Is that such a great idea?"

"All that trouble is in the past," I said, hoping it was true. "I'll call you when I get back. How's that drunken Irish husband of yours?"

"Kevin is fine. He asked me to ask you why you don't come up to Woodstock any more."

"Tell him it's because I can't stand seeing you with another man."

"Kevin will be so pleased to hear that. He thought you didn't care."

"Katie, why don't you get rid of that guy and come back to me?"

"You just say that to be gallant. For one thing, you're still with Mylar."

"That's only temporary," I told her, "until Sheldon makes the big decision and takes her away. Kate, you know it's always been you."

Katie laughed. "Hobart, when are you going to take life seriously? You know very well that if I showed the slightest inclination to come back to you, you'd run like a thief in the night."

"You might have something there. Tell you what, why don't you and I have one last mad fling at this little hotel I know in Miami?"

"Sure, if I can bring Kevin."

"I didn't know he's a pervert."

"He's not. He just likes to talk. He'd probably have a lot to say about something like that."

"Kate, I don't think you're taking me seriously."

"My dear, you forget that I lived with you for ten years. I ought to know by now when not to take you seriously."

"And when not to take me at all."

"I learned that, too, yes," Katie said. "You're really going to Paris?"

"That's right."

"Hob, take care of yourself. Don't try to prove anything. And for your own sake, try to stay out of Ibiza."

"All I'm doing is trying to earn a living," I told her. "I pay you support, you'll remember, despite the rapidly increasing wealth of your shyster lawyer husband."

"Stop that," Katie said. "Supporting the kids has nothing to do with Kevin. It doesn't matter how much he makes. They're yours and mine."

"I know that. Only kidding. I'll call you when I'm back."

"Hob," she said, "how are things with you and Mylar?"

"The same," I said.

"Is Sheldon still living with you?"

"Yep."

"Really, Hob, that's tacky; you shouldn't put up with it."

"What can I do? They're in love."

"Then they should move out of your house and find their own place."

"The trouble is, neither of them is sure exactly what he or she wants to do. I don't know if Mylar's quite ready to set up housekeeping with Sheldon, and he's not going to leave until she says she will."

"It's a hopeless mess," Katie said. "Why on earth did you ever get involved with a woman named Mylar?"

"It seemed a good idea at the time," I said.

These are the words that I expect to have carved on my tombstone.

SHELDON 7

MY APARTMENT ON State Street is one half of a frame house painted a color you can't quite identify and forget as soon as you turn away from it. I went in and stood a moment in the dark, narrow hallway. "Mylar?" I called.

"She's not here," a voice said from the parlor.

It's one of those houses with a parlor and a bay window. Mylar and I rent out the attic room. Sheldon was sitting in the parlor. Sheldon is short and intense, a stocky, vaguely Assyrian-looking man with tightly waved black hair. Features a trifle heavy. Mouth a little droopy. Fixed smile frequently on face. Not the sort of person I'd go for, personally, but of course I'm not the one who picked him.

"Where'd she go?" I asked.

"She said she'd be right back." There was something fishy about the way he said it.

"All right, but where'd she go to?"

"Nowhere in particular," Sheldon said. He paused, then blurted, "She just wanted to give us a little time together."

I stared at him. "What on earth do you and I need any time together for?"

"To try to work things out," Sheldon said.

"Oh, no, Sheldon," I said. "Not now. Not *things.* I'm tired. I've got a client. The initial interview took a lot out of me."

"A good-paying client?" Sheldon asked, momentarily brightening.

"No. Just a normal deadbeat client like the usual kind I get."

Sheldon stood up, walked up and down the room pounding his right fist into the palm of his left hand. I believe he was portraying frustrated anger. Or maybe angry frustration. In any case, he turned to me after a moment and said, "Damn it, Hob, this can't go on."

"My sentiments exactly. Does that mean you're going away?" Sheldon lives with us due to a concatenation of circumstances too ridiculous to be chronicled, and tangential, in any event, to my story. But I see that now, having mentioned them at all, I must explain.

I met Sheldon five years ago, when the I.R.S. (on whose name be peace) audited me. After an exchange of paperwork, they sent Sheldon from the Newark office to look over my records. After spending a few hours going through the sackful of paper I dumped in his lap, some of them on the sort of extremely flimsy paper that Ibicenco shopkeepers used in the days when I lived in Ibiza and accumulated these pieces of paper, he looked up in annoyance. "Mr. Draconian"—we were still quite formal at that stage—"don't you have any better records than these?"

"I'm not so good about pieces of paper," I told him. "I try to keep them all: I know that Uncle Sammy wants me to. But they get lost; you know what I mean, man? But you might ask my wife, Mylar; she may have some old cash ledgers; I believe she's sentimental about things like that."

And then, pat upon the moment, Mylar entered. Five feet nine, slender, pointy-breasted, svelte-legged Mylar of the radiant smile and china-blue eyes. Sheldon saw (as he told me afterwards) the fulfillment of his most impossible boyhood dreams when he beheld this beautiful, outrageous lady in skintight jeans, sequined blouse, snakeskin boots, cowboy hat, clunky jewelry, crazy makeup, with purple streak in her hair. It was love at first sight, he confessed to me months later over too many beers in

McGinty's on Grit Street down near Macadam. For him she represented the impossible dream.

To be honest about it, Sheldon's sudden interest in my wife was not entirely unwelcome; I had been wondering how to get rid of Mylar. Not that there was anything wrong with her. She was just crazy in her way and I was crazy in mine, and we had drifted so far apart that only the cosmic interrelatedness of everything gave us anything at all in common. And here was this nice fellow with high moral standards and a steady job, who was going to take her off my hands so that I could jettison my other responsibilities as well, sell the house and go live *my* impossible dream, namely, to return to Europe and find the magic again. They say you can never do it twice; once is all you get, and if you don't like once try none, the other option; but I can dream, can't I?

There was a difficulty, however. I was Sheldon's case and he'd staked his reputation and pride on this one, and the only thing that would satisfy his exquisitely well-honed sense of ethics was to bring my case to successful completion; that is, to collect Uncle Sammy's due for the dinero I had somehow failed to fork over in previous years even less successful than this one. Only then would he feel the moral right, the *certitude,* I believe he called it, to allow him without guilt to take my wife.

Well, shucks, I'm not a bad guy, and I'd just as soon have paid up to government. I just didn't have the money, that's all. There are the payments to Katie and the kids. There's rent on my office. There's this and there's that, and never enough for everything.

But I remembered a time once, long ago, when I had lived without money, or without the anxiety of it, on a magic island where no one starved and you couldn't bomb out because you were Home, in the great good place where everyone looked out for everyone else.

That is fantasy, of course, or rather, delusion; but what can I do; that's how I feel about it, and a man needs a dream even if it's chimaerical.

I had, of course, some residual feeling for Mylar, whom I had found myself married to after an unsuccessful attempt on state-of-the-art drugs to find The Supreme Unity that unifies Apparent Diversity. You can wind up in some surprising places on these new hallucinogenics. Like standing before a justice of the peace in Leesville, North Carolina. You say you've had your own experiences along that line? Yes, but you didn't wake up and find yourself married to a woman who called herself Mylar and had a streak of purple dyed in her hair, and who was zanily and cheerfully impossible, especially for one whose favorite pastime is feeling sorry for himself.

That was six months ago. Now here we were, in a pleasant little trap of our own devising. Sheldon had moved out of his apartment in Hoboken and rented our attic bedroom when it became available. It was a little tough on Sheldon's conscience that Sheldon and Mylar simply stay apart any longer. But they also couldn't sleep with each other, at least in Sheldon's view, because that would have turned a nicely ripening tragedy into a domestic farce, and you get no points for idiot roles in the reviews which self-appreciation publishes daily. No, you gets no bread with one meatball and so Sheldon and Mylar lived sexlessly, with the attendant augmentation of desire so often noted in circumstances of enforced chastity, until the very walls steamed with their contained and pressurized lust, and I took to spending a lot of time in my office or at the movies because, despite my best attempts, I was not *entirely* a removed observer.

"Now listen to me," Sheldon said. "You must resolve this thing. You must get some money together and pay the government, so I can close this case and take Mylar away from here to my new position."

"What new position?"

"Didn't I tell you? I'm next in line to become Senior Auditor at our Morristown facility."

"Congratulations," I said. "You'll make a great auditor. And Mylar will make a great Mrs. Auditor. I assume your intentions toward her are still honorable?"

"Of course they're honorable," Sheldon said. "I want Mylar to divorce you so I can marry her and take her to Morristown with me. But I can't do anything until I close your case."

"I don't see why not," I said. "The Home Office won't hold one unclosed case against you."

"I'm not worried about the Home Office," Sheldon said. "The fact is my own conscience won't permit me to take the promotion and your wife until I've closed your file. I guess I'm just an old-fashioned, inner-directed sort of guy, and there's nothing I can do about it." He laughed with the false self-deprecation of a man well pleased with himself. I could have kicked him.

Still, on the bright side, Sheldon's character gave me an avenue of escape from the constrictions of my life with Mylar. Pay the money, Draconian, and so win freedom. But where to find the money?

"Maybe I'll make something on this case," I told him. "I'll be leaving for Paris in a couple of days."

"You're going to Paris?" Sheldon said.

"Yes, of course," I said. "That's where this case is taking me. You and Mylar have a good time while I'm gone, hear?" I gave him a suggestive leer. It's not that I get off on that sort of thing, but I wanted to encourage him because I knew that when Mylar deigned to sleep with a dude, he didn't get away. I hadn't.

MILLIE 8

I WENT OVER to Millie's loft on Water Street so she could arrange the air fares. Millie's an old friend from Ibiza. I let myself in with my key. Millie was in bed asleep, lying on her back and snoring noisily, resembling a pink baby whale in a blue nightie. One of the things she brought back from Ibiza, aside from a big floppy Formentera hat and two pairs of sandals from the Sandal Shop at the beginning of the Dalt Vila, was a nasty habit with Quaaludes.

I try to put all my friends into the Alternative Detective Agency. My international organization is made up mostly of friends from various periods of my life. Some of them are former hippies. A lot of them were a lot of other things. Our paths crossed in Ibiza, one of the main stops on the exile's circuit.

One advantage of living abroad is that you end up with friends everywhere. The only difficulty is trying to figure out how to use them. I figured I was performing a social service, opening up trade to people who usually don't get it. Down with the big grifters; let the small ones get into the action. Don't go Hertz or Avis; try out our very own Nosedive Motors. Let our Haitian Brigade paint your house.

We need the work, we exiles. We are the third-worlders of western civilization. Believe me, you don't have to be black or Hispanic to feel disinherited and disenfranchised in America in the closing years of the twentieth century.

It hasn't anything to do with politics, race or religion. There are a lot of bright, personable people who are being hammered into the ground because they don't fit, because they aren't a part of the growing obsolescence of everything that was ever worth having.

That is the reasoning behind the Alternative Detective Agency. It's sort of a commune. We don't call it that, of course. "Commune" for most people calls up an image of pretty, long-haired girls performing loathsome sex with skinheaded freaks with crankcase grease impacted under their fingernails. Whereas my organization tries to exude an image of normal Americans engaged in the national pastime, Making Money Any Which Way You Can.

The Alternative Detective Agency is the holding company for me and my people. We've got branches all over the world, wherever one of my old Ibiza friends happens to be living. They help me solve my cases and I cut them in on the profits, if any. If there aren't any, we get high and talk about old times.

They are my people, and they inhabit my real country, the exile's misty kingdom of memories and displacements. They are wanderers and vagrants, artists and would-be artists, con men and remittance men, students of the university of perpetual reeducation, a floating English-speaking society that travels south to San Tropez and Ibiza in the summer and north to Paris, London and Amsterdam in the winter, like herds of delicate reindeer crossing Ice-Age Europe.

Everybody has heard of ludes, those little white pills that make you feel very good unless they kill you. Not everyone knows what Quaaludin does. First of all, you have to take it on an empty stomach, so the little white pill can dissolve quickly and get through the stomach wall into your bloodstream. If you put a lot of food in its way you can't expect a good hit.

And of course the lude doesn't always come on. Usually it'll work, but sometimes something goes wrong, something to do with body chemistry, maybe, and the lude just doesn't take. And that's a tough one, because that's when you start getting strung out.

I'd had the habit for a while myself. The first thing you notice is that your face has turned to rubber. After that, it really gets good. The price, unfortunately, is that the junk stays in your system a long time, twenty-four hours at least, so you don't function so good the next day after a pill. And if you take one or more every night, like I used to do, you end up not functioning well any of the time. Another of Quaaludin's side effects is its tendency to form stones in a user's kidney. Passing a kidney stone is the male equivalent of difficult childbirth.

I shook Millie into consciousness. She's a big woman, with streaks of gray in her shoulder-length brown hair. Nice looking still, and competent, too, despite her habit. I got her to understand what I wanted: two round trip fares to Paris, open end, cheapest possible way. Try one of the courier services. I also wrote it all down so that she'd know what this was about when she woke up again, after going back to sleep when I left as she inevitably would.

I left then and started back to my office. As I was passing the Thom McAn Shoe Store, I caught a reflection in the window and realized I was being followed. Across the street, a portly man in a dark blue suit was loitering. Come to think of it, I'd seen him earlier, too.

I started walking and by discreet use of the reflecting surfaces of cars and windows ascertained that he was still behind me, ambling with too casual an air. I came around Argyll Street and quickly circled the block, hoping to jump out at him from behind. But when I came around the corner again, he was gone.

I tried to think of all the people who might be following me. After fifteen names, I gave up. But it bothered me. It had been ten years since I'd been in Europe last. After the Turkish thing, it had seemed wiser to stay away.

But what the hell, that had been long ago, and not my fault, anyhow, not really. And you can't spend the rest of your life avoiding Europe. Not if you're Hob Draconian.

Paris, queen of cities. And the rest of Europe. Hob's Europe: Ibiza, Majorca, Barcelona, London, Amsterdam, Athens, and the islands of the central Cyclades. And Rome, incomparable Rome.

How I longed to see them again. All that stood in the way was the memory of a day ten years ago, in the Ankara airport.

It had been hot as hell that day. August in Turkey. The airport was crowded, and there were plenty of tourists. We had been counting on that. We had done this before; everything was going to go all right.

Then why this apprehension, this tingling panic, this sensation of having bitten down on an ice-cold toad? What was wrong with me; what subtle clue had jangled my alarm system; why was my head full of snapshots of Turkish prisons?

Just as I reached the emigration booth, I saw Lieutenant Jarosik bulging out of his starched khakis, his black moustache a neat triangle against his sweaty olive cheek. My response was unconscious, automatic. I turned like a marionette, noting that he hadn't noticed me yet. I walked steadily out of the airport without a backward glance and got into a taxi. I took it down to the docks and caught the last ferry across the Bosphorus to the European side.

I can't really explain why I did that. Jarosik didn't have anything on me. But he wasn't the sort of man to hang out in the airport checking people as they passed through. I knew that something had gone wrong; somebody had talked. I knew they had called in Jarosik because he knew me by sight, as he also knew Jean-Claude and Nigel.

Once in European Turkey, I joined a sight-seeing tour to the ruins of Edirne. After that I made a normal crossing through the checkpoint into Greece. Took a taxi to Komotini, and then trains and busses to Athens.

Two days later, while I was having a beer in the George V in Syntagma Square, I saw a story on page five of the *International Herald-Tribune.* A Frenchman and a Britisher had been seized at customs in the Istanbul airport.

They found the hashish, of course. The false bottoms I'd built into the Samsonites couldn't stand up to the sort of inspection the customs people give when they know what they're looking for.

The trial was held later that month, and they gave Jean-Claude and Nigel life sentences. But those were reduced to two years when their lawyer proved that they were innocently carrying the suitcases for a third man—Mr. Big—name withheld—who was also supposed to get on the flight but had evidently panicked at the last moment.

Some money changed hands, and my friends were out in a year. But they were angry, so I was told. And they blamed the mishap on me. In fact, they had been quite abusive about it, even threatening. But that had been ten years ago.

I had tried to carry on with my life. I was a professional poker player in those days, not of the first rank, but good enough for the competition you encountered in Europe. The main action was never in the casinos, although you could make a living at them. The real poker action was at private parties, and in the hotel rooms of the rich at Cannes, Nice, Rome. The games were easy to beat. What was difficult was to lose often enough so they'd continue inviting you.

It called for walking a certain line. You had to *appear* not to win too much. When you lost, you called attention to it: valuable publicity. You kept track of your real wins and losses in a lined school composition book. You kept that money separate from the rest. When it was possible. Although sometimes you and Katie had to eat on winnings. Then you played on paper, praying it would work out, reestablishing your nut, as they called the poker stake, when you won again.

It was a tightrope, but at least I knew what I was doing. Until I started losing. Then I tightened up, began to make bad moves, errors of judgment, trying to get even, trying to win. And the drugs didn't help, either.

And then it all started falling apart.

Panic, paranoia, cold flashes, bad ideas, and The Fear.

And so I came back to America. And now I was going back to Europe again.

After Turkey I realized that life was not a dream. I realized I was playing with dangerous stuff. Everybody smuggled in those days. I hadn't really believed I could get caught. That's because I'd gotten used to the warm glow of safety and invulnerability that drugs can give you, especially ludes, when sweet lassitude floods you and your face goes numb and you sink into a twilight place called The Way You Like It.

Well, that was then and now was now. I was off the stuff; the past was buried in Père Lachaise cemetery with my hero, Jim Morrison, and I was returning to Paris.

MARIA GUASCH 9

Harry Hamm wasn't feeling so good the morning my detailed cable reached him. He was feeling a little flat. The first flush of pleasure at being on the island had passed. He had fixed up his house, applied for his *permanencia,* the papers you need to reside in Spain as a full-time resident. His garden was doing nicely, he had some friends. But something was missing, and he wasn't sure what.

He told me he had been glad to get my cable, because at this point he was ready to do anything, just to be occupied.

He started up his SEAT and drove the twenty minute trip to the port of Ibiza. He spent a lot of time walking around, looking for Industrias Marisol. He finally found it, a little sailboard and scuba gear shop tucked into an alleyway off the Calle de la Virgen. The shop was closed.

Harry walked around for a while, peering in the window, wondering what to do next. It was a fine day, the port was humming—it was June, fine weather, tourists arriving every day, a big season coming up by July.

After a while an old Ibicencan in a shoe repair shop across the street noticed him trying to peer in the window.

"Are you looking for Vico?"

"This his store?"

"Yes, Vico and his brother, Enrique."

"Where can I find them?"

"Enrique left the island last night. Flew to San Sebastián, so I heard. As for Vico, he's gone fishing with the Guasch brothers."

"Will they be back soon?"

The old Ibicencan shrugged. *"¿Quién sabé?"*

"Don't the fishing boats usually come in around sunset?"

"The ones tourists hire, yes. But the Guasch brothers are commercial fishermen. No telling how long they'll be away."

"Is there some way I could get in contact with them?"

The shoemaker laughed. "You could ask a sea gull."

Antonio grinned, then turned away, his eyes going sly. Harry recognized it, the island look, don't tell the outsiders anything.

"What about their business? Who looks after things when they're away?

"Maria Guasch, of course. Their sister."

Harry wrote down the directions and went to Maria's finca in Santa Gertrudis.

Maria's place was a small, scrupulously kept farm in the hills near Santa Gertrudis. The low stone house was one of the old-fashioned fincas, built in accord with the length of the ridgepole, which was the longest piece of seasoned oak obtainable. There were two fields of almond trees. A few acres for crops such as cabbages and potatoes. Spaced neatly in the middle of the fields were the *algorobos,* the carob trees whose pods the Ibicencans dry and grind and feed to their animals in winter. A dog announced Harry's arrival. It was one of those long, lean, yellow-eyed Ibicencan hounds that have been part of the island history since the time of the Carthaginians.

Harry parked on a shoulder of the lane that ran in front of the farm. A woman had come outside and was standing just in front of the doorway, shading her eyes with one hand, looking at him. Harry called out, *"¿Con permiso?"* When she nodded he opened the gate and walked to the farmhouse.

The woman was an Ibicenca, but her clothing was not the unrelieved black of the older island women. She still wore the long full skirt and long-sleeved blouse and little jacket. The women of Ibiza had been dressing like this for centuries. But the material of her skirt was a patterned brown and white rather than black, and her blouse was cream-colored with little figures. Her features were strong and beautiful. Her hair was black and straight, lustrous, tied back in a knot at the nape of her neck. She was tall for a woman of the islands, and slender. There was a serenity about her that Harry liked. She seemed to be in her late thirties or early forties.

Harry introduced himself. In the Ibicencan fashion he told the woman where he lived, and how long he'd been on the island. He explained that he was looking into a problem for a friend, a problem which concerned a shipment sent to Señor Vico at Industrias Marisol and not paid for. He had just learned that Señor Vico had gone fishing with the Guasch brothers. Harry wondered if she knew where they had gone and when they'd be back.

"They didn't tell me anything about this," Maria said. "But sometimes Pablo and César go fishing and stay out for several days at a time. Sometimes they put into a mainland port to refuel and stay a few days. They could be gone a week or more."

"And you don't know where they were going this time?"

"No," she said. But he could see that it was bothering her, Vico going along with them, and maybe she was wondering like Harry was what Vico had brought along for the ride. Five sailboards, maybe, fully equipped, to flog off somewhere along the Côte d'Azur?

"Is there anybody who might know where your brothers went?"

"The fishermen know everything about each other," she told him. "You could ask on the docks. But they won't tell you anything."

"Well," Harry said, "thanks for your help. I guess I'd better try."

Maria hesitated. She was looking at him curiously. Then she asked him if he would like a glass of water. Harry said he'd like that very much. She offered him a seat in the shade of the porch, under the grape arbor. She went in and brought him a glass of water.

"Hey," Harry said, after a couple of sips, "this is some water!"

Maria looked pleased. "It's from the well on my grandfather's farm, across the island behind San Juan. It's the best water on the island."

"Well, it's great. Thanks." He finished the glass and put it down on the porch, stood up.

"My brothers are not in any trouble, are they?" Maria asked.

"Not that I know of," Harry said. "But if they're smuggling stolen goods out of Spain they could get into some trouble."

"You think that Vico has stolen these boards and is using my brothers to transport them somewhere?"

"It looks that way," Harry said.

"Wait a minute," she said. "My brothers may smuggle a little whiskey or cigarettes, just like all the fishermen. There have been *contrabandistas* in these islands for centuries. But my brothers would never transport stolen goods."

"Maybe they don't know those boards are stolen," Harry said. "Maybe they're just taking them somewhere for Vico like general cargo."

Maria thought about it, then went inside the finca. She came out almost at once with a black kerchief around her hair and a shawl around her shoulders.

"I will come with you and speak to the men on the docks. You'll get nowhere otherwise. Somebody may know where my brothers went."

FLIGHT TO PARIS 10

RACHEL TOLD ME a little about herself during the flight to Paris. She claimed to be the only daughter of short parents, but had herself grown to the height of five feet nine, the tallest occurrence in her family in almost a hundred years. She had gone to high school in Waukegan, Illinois, and movingly described to me the cold winters they used to have, and how in February the neighborhood dogs, turning wild, began to run in packs and bring down the occasional delivery man. She told me how her father, a Church of England minister, had turned to repairing McCormick reapers when his entire congregation, a family of twenty-three from Little Dorking in Hampshire, moved to Hawaii.

We entertained each other with lies and ambiguous glances as the plane trudged eastward above the corrugated gray Atlantic. The sun went down and the movie came up, a comedy starring George Burns as Tamerlane. I grew thoughtful after a while, thinking back over the faces in the crowd of people watching the departure, wondering if I hadn't spotted the large man of the previous day.

After a while, the movie ended and the stewardess brought coffee. Rachel fell asleep with the cup in her hand resting against the plastic passenger tray. I put it away for her and then fell asleep myself. I woke up when the "Fasten Seatbelts" announcement came on. We were on our final approach to De Gaulle Airport.

3

ARRIVAL IN PARIS 11

RACHEL WAS IMPRESSED by everything, especially the way everybody talked French and looked foreign. As for me, I felt like I'd come home. I had my own Paris, made up of the Rue Mouffetard, the Rue du Bac, the Rue du Cygne; the cafés along St-Germain-des-Prés, with their starched white linen tablecloths set against rows of amber mirrors in which tuxedoed waiters glided beneath cut-glass chandeliers, the whole bathed in a rosy Belle Époque glow; the weird stone landscapes of Châtelet-les-Halles; the hi-fi section of the FNAC store in Montparnasse; the Tex-Mex restaurant in a cobblestoned courtyard below a dance studio on the Rue du Temple; the American library near the Tour Eiffel; the science-fiction bookstore on the Boulevard St-Jacques.

We went through customs and immigration. The polite French police official stamped our passports with indifferent benevolence: your papers are in order, you're in Paris, everything is going to be all right.

The taxi into town was expensive, but what the hell, it was Rachel's money. I gave the taxi an address in the seventh arrondissement. My French was rusty, but I got through OK. The French are intelligent enough to figure out almost any attempt you make in their language. Of course, my driver was an Algerian named Mohammed ben-Amouk, so maybe things *had* changed a little since I was there last.

The ride into Paris from De Gaulle was familiar and comforting. The modern dual concrete highway went across flat fields, farm land, and then an area of light industry as we approached Paris. Then more arterial highways began feeding in and we were at the Porte de la Chapelle, entering the Périphérique that circles Paris.

It was still morning. I had planned that we would check in first with my old buddy Rus. Rus is a light-skinned Negro from the Caribbean, Jamaica or Barbados; his story changes over the years. The way Rus tells it, he had worked his passage to America as a kid, lived in Key West and Miami for a while, managed to join the American army in time for World War II, lived through the Normandy campaign, and had taken his discharge in Paris. He met Rosemary, a pretty blonde Dutch girl studying art history, and they married. Rus never left France again, except for summer holidays on Ibiza. Dutch girls make the best wives of any European nationality, in my humble opinion. Rosemary spoke English better than Rus, in a marked New Jersey accent. But if you listened carefully you could hear the shading of "th" sounds to "d", a remnant of her native accent.

The taxi came into the Boulevard St-Germain and took a left turn down the Rue de Bellechasse.

"Well, well," Rosemary said, looking at me when she opened the door, "look what the cat dragged in. Long time between drinks, huh, Hob?"

She led us in through the tiny kitchenette.

Rus's apartment was dark and tiny and crowded with furniture. There was a bright Mexican blanket on the queen-size bed which they used for a couch by day. Near the bed was an ornamental brass table from Morocco with a tall brass hookah on it. In the corner of the room was the little drawing table with a gooseneck lamp, where Rus did his sketching, the radio close to him. There were a few original sketches on the walls, the work of friends of his. The room had a homey smell of wine, black tobacco, and the Sunday roast.

Rosemary had broadened out some in the years since I'd seen her last, but she still was a very attractive lady—ample, open-faced, her flaxen hair beginning to gray, her smile as cheerful as ever.

"Rosemary," I said, "I'd like you to meet my client, Miss Rachel Starr."

"Hi," Rosemary said, "any client of Hob Draconian is a friend of mine. How's the Alternative Detective Agency, Hob?"

"I'm here on Agency business," I said. "And all my friends are going to get a piece of the action."

"It's not really very big action," Rachel explained. "I can't afford much, though maybe we can figure out a bonus at the end if everything goes all right."

"Nobody expects to make anything out of the Agency," Rosemary said. "It just gives us something to talk about."

Rus and Rosemary lived in a small apartment at 6, Rue de Bellechasse, not far from Invalides and the Chambre de Deputies. It was one of those rent-controlled Paris apartments that still exist, even in the high-rent districts, to reward those who don't move. It was rumored that Leslie Caron lived in this building, though nobody had actually seen her.

Rus was the same as always, a huge, soft, caramel-colored butterball of a man, hunched over his drawing board in a corner of the living room, drawing cartoons all day to the accompaniment of a whisper of jazz from his radio. He got up to greet me, enfolding me in the big *abrazado* that Ibiza exiles share when they meet.

We sat down over a couple of Stella d'Artois beers and discussed old times and new. Rus was a center for news and information about Ibiza and its far-ranging exiles. Rus and Rosemary held an open house every Sunday. It was what the French call *un bouf,* an eating. He was a quick and inventive cook, Rus was, renowned for his miniature Mexican pizzas and baby spare-ribs.

Rus and I had both known Alex back in the old Ibiza days. At that time, Alex had been a young lawyer who dropped out for a taste of la dolce vita Ibiza-style. After a while he had returned to a practice in Washington, D.C., and that's the last I'd heard of him.

From Rachel I had learned that Alex had been working for the Selwyn Corporation, professional fundraisers for various causes, some of them legitimate. It was at this time that he had met Rachel. They had been planning to go to Europe together. Alex had gone over first. He had been playing with a combo in Paris, Les Monstres Sacrés, a sort of hobby with him; he loved the raffish Paris music scene. Shortly after his arrival, he had disappeared or dropped out of contact.

Rus hadn't heard anything; Alex hadn't gotten in touch with him during this most recent visit.

The place to begin the search was with Alex's combo. They were playing at a café called El Mango Encantado, on Rue Gregory l'Angevin near the Centre Pompidou. Rosemary, whose French is a lot better than mine, telephoned one of my favorite little hotels, Le Cygne, on the Rue du Cygne near the Beaubourg. We booked Rachel separately into the Crillon, a famous luxury-class hotel in the first arrondissement. For a girl with limited funds, she was doing all right for herself. But what the hell, first time in Paris is the time to go for it. It was close to the Louvre, she explained to me. That was where she was planning to spend her time while I looked for Alex.

EL MANGO ENCANTADO 12

RACHEL AND I walked east on the Boulevard St-Germain, then north on the Boulevard St-Michel, across the Seine by way of the Pont St-Michel, and across the Île de la Cité, catching a glimpse of Notre-Dame as we entered the Boulevard Sébastopol on the Right Bank.

El Mango Encantado was on the Rue des Blancs not far from the Centre Pompidou. It was one of the many South American café-restaurants that had opened recently to cater to the increasing numbers of South American students and exiles, who were such a part of the current Paris scene. It was a small dimly lit place where you could hang out all day over a glass of wine. Nearby was the Beaubourg, the great art museum and library founded by Arne Pompidou. This was a very mixed area, a combination of old and new, ancient and modern, and, in Baudrillard's phrase, the hypermodern.

The combo was just setting up. The leader, Marcello, was pointed out to me, a curly-headed Uruguayan who was also their piano player. I asked him if I could buy him a drink.

Over a Cinzano, Marcello told me that Alex had been staying in a flat on the Boulevard Auguste-Blanqui in the thirteenth arrondissement.

"Do you know the thirteenth?" he asked. "There's a big shopping mall in the Place d'Italie. I'd meet Alex at a restaurant there, a place called Roszes. He was always late. I'd walk around the shopping mall, waiting for him, watching the old dames with their dogs and having an occasional apéritif. I didn't see him when he came down from Amsterdam, however. Juanito was with him, though. Hey, Juanito, what can you tell this fellow about Alex?"

Juanito was the drummer, a small, big-chested fellow with Indian features and heavy horn-rimmed glasses. He had been the son of a diplomat in Chile before Pinochet.

"Sure, I met him at the Gare du Nord when he came down from Amsterdam. We had lunch together at the Café Tranquilité on the Rue Simon-le-Franc. You know the place, near the Place des Innocents where the dope dealers hang out."

I knew the place. The art students of the Beaubourg use it frequently. And of course the tourists. These streets are closed to traffic, though an occasional car does get through, this being Paris, and pokes its way through the crowds like a hippo tiptoeing through the tulips.

Juanito continued. "I think Alex was waiting for somebody. He put down his newspaper every few minutes and looked right and left. Then some guy I've never seen before comes up and whispers something to him and goes away.

"Alex excuses himself and says he has to see someone. I've never seen Alex act like this. I haven't got anything on that afternoon, so I follow him.

"He goes to Goldenberg's on the Rue Vieille-de-Temple. That's the kosher place where you can get overboiled beef with horseradish, just like in New York or Warsaw. I didn't want him to catch me watching him, because Alex is a little funny about that sort of thing. I had a falafel sandwich at one of the Jewish places nearby and waited. And I wondered, because this really wasn't his sort of place. Alex went in for places like the Crazy Horse Saloon, or the Tex-Mex place on the Boulevard Montparnasse. And he loved to go for tea at the Café Deux Magots on St-Germain. The place where Sartre used to have his famous quarrels with Simone de Beauvoir."

Juanito's mention of Deux-Magots reminded me of a story an American girl had told me about how she met Jean-Paul Sartre.

She said she had been having a Coke in Le Café Deux Magots because it was so famous, and she had recognized Sartre from a smudged reproduction on the back of one of the American editions of *L'Etre et le néant.* She told me that Sartre looked like a toad dressed in black, but beautiful.

She was a California girl. It was second nature for her to go over to his table and ask for his autograph. Sartre asked her to join him and Miss Simone de Beauvoir. My friend said she didn't like to cause Miss de Beauvoir pain, as her joining the table was very obviously going to do, to judge by the martyred expression Miss de Beauvoir put on when Sartre made the invitation. But what the hell, this was going to be a world-class anecdote and Mr. Sartre and his lady friend probably had this sort of problem all the time. She sat down and Sartre bought her a Coke, and asked how she was enjoying Paris, and groped her under the table, so she thought he was kind of sweet and considered hanging around long enough to ball him so she'd have a *super* world-class anecdote. But she wasn't really as tough as all that; sometimes she just liked to scare herself, and besides, she and the other kids were bicycling to Tours in the morning and she needed her sleep.

Her story had great point for me. It's what I call the human side of philosophy.

Juanito was saying, "Alex came out of Goldenberg's after a while and caught a taxi. I caught one immediately after. It was a day made for surveillance. 'Follow that taxi!' I said to the driver.

" 'There's a twenty franc surcharge for following people,' the driver says to me, swinging away from the curb. Like he was reminding me of a local statute.

" 'Done!' I said, and away we went.

"We followed him to the Gare Montparnasse. There I lost him. That's all I can tell you."

I thanked Juanito, then asked Marcello whether he knew of anyone else I could speak to concerning Alex.

"Sure," he said. "The obvious person to contact would be Gerard Clovis."

"Who's that?"

"The film director. Surely you've heard of him?"

"Oh, that Gerard Clovis," I said.

"It's true that he's not too well known outside France, but he's got a lot of prestige here. Clovis is picking up where Goddard left off, so to speak."

"What does he have to do with Alex?"

"I thought you knew. Alex was working for him."

"As what?"

"An actor. He and Clovis met at a party, and Clovis thought he'd be perfect for a part in his new film."

ARNE 13

IT DIDN'T TAKE too long for me to find out that Gerard Clovis worked out of the Gaumont movie studios in the north of Paris. I telephoned from a street corner phone booth. No answer. I had forgotten it was lunchtime in Paris, the sacred hour. I decided to ask a few questions around Beaubourg-Les Halles. This was Alex's turf, a city within a city. I was bound to find someone who knew something.

I left Rachel in a café near the entrance to the Beaubourg, where she had a good view of the fire- and glass-eaters who perform in the sunken flagstoned courtyard at the front of the museum. She planned to lunch there, then spend a few hours in the Beaubourg to see the Dali exhibit, then go back to the Crillon. I told her I'd call her there.

It was good to be walking in Paris on a bright June day, the streets filled with tourists and lovers. I had lunch at Le Disque Bleu, a students' place on the Rue Rambuteau. The onion soup was a meal in itself, and I followed it with a duck pâté sandwich on crusty French bread. A café crème completed it, and I left to continue my stroll.

I walked around L'Éspace Baltard, where the new sports complex is being built, then once around the Forum des Halles, and so to the Fountain of Innocents, around which Africans with embroidered caps sell leather drums and brass jewelry. This part of Paris always wears a carnival face. Then I spotted a mime working the crowd, watched him for a moment, and remembered that I knew him.

Arne the mime had the classic white-painted Marcel Marceau face, the black lines from forehead to cheek down the middle of the eye, the painted rosebud mouth. He had a simple but effective routine. When people passed, engrossed in conversation, Arne would fall into step behind them, mimicking their movements, exaggerating them, to humorous effect but without malice. When the people he was mimicking realized he was there, Arne in dumb show, would invite them to follow him. Sometimes he'd get a conga line of five or ten people capering around imitating him. Arne was very good and when he passed the hat, people were generous. He made a good thing out of it. He was a Dane, in his mid-thirties, small and tightly muscled, and he moved with a dancer's grace.

He spotted me, came over and sat down at my table on the sidewalk. We exchanged *ça va*'s. I ordered a Cinzano and he accepted a lemonade.

"So you have come back," Arne said. "Is that really smart, Hob?"

"Come on," I said. "That stuff went down a long time ago. And it wasn't my fault."

Arne shrugged, a habit he'd picked up in France. "None of my business, anyway. What are you doing here?"

"I'm trying to find a guy," I told him. "You knew him, too, back in the old Ibiza days. Alex Sinclair."

"Yeah, he was around here. But I haven't seen him in a couple weeks, maybe longer."

"Do you know a movie director named Gerard Clovis?"

"Of course. People say he's the new Fellini."

"I hear Alex is working in one of his films."

Arne raised one eyebrow. Another French habit he'd picked up. A bead of sweat ran down his white face and rolled down to the blue bandanna knotted around his neck.

"Yes," he said, "Alex is participating in one of Clovis' films.

Perhaps 'acting' is too strong a term for what Clovis wants. He likes to set up situations, then throw his people into them without preparation. Sometimes he will give certain lines and actions to one or two of his actors, but never to all of them. And he never reveals who has the planned lines and who is supposed to be improvising freely."

"I haven't heard of the guy," I told him.

"Here in France he's known as the Erik Satie of cinematography."

"Is that good?"

"Here in France, it's very good indeed."

"Nice guy?"

"In a way. Also sarcastic, childlike, and a believer in miracles. Like Fellini, an assembler of cameras and crews on the streets. Cinema Verité stuff. The story is false but the faces are real."

"You don't know what the movie's about?"

"No one does, not even Clovis. Clovis likes to work in a free, unplanned, unstructured, unpremeditated way. The impromptu has great charm for Clovis. From the start he's been against the cult of actors, and against Stanislavskian method, too. In fact, he is opposed to the whole ideal of artistic portrayal. He wants to assemble movies out of a collage of faces, movements and sequences."

"When does he start filming?"

"Probably within the week. Would you like to meet him? Come to the rehearsal tomorrow and I'll introduce you. Clovis loves foreigners."

We arranged a time to meet at the Café des Innocents. I paid for the drinks and went back to my hotel room.

I have noticed that private detectives in fiction tend to be much more active than their counterparts in real life. I suppose I could have followed up a few more leads that day. But frankly, I was tired. I lay down for a nap.

TONY ROMAGNA 14

THAT EVENING, AS I was walking from the hotel to meet Rachel, I saw him again. There simply could be no doubt of it. The shape, the dark suit with the bright red gardenia in the buttonhole, the broad, dark, good-natured face. It was the man who had been following me in Snuff's Landing, and here he was in Paris.

The guy had paused near the entrance to FNAC. He was lighting a cigar. I walked up to him and said, "Well, well, small world, isn't it?"

He finished lighting his cigar deliberately, then gave me a cool look. "Have we met before?" he asked in good New Jersey English.

"Probably not," I said. "But I'm sure you know who I am."

He looked amused. "Why should I?"

"Because you were following me in the States, and you're following me here."

"Coincidence," he said, looking right at me and grinning. He was saying, in body English, Sure, I've been following you; what are you going to do about it?

"Just to make it easy for you," I said, "my name is Hobart Draconian and I'm staying right near here at the Hôtel Cygne, on the Rue du Cygne. You probably already know that, but I just thought I'd confirm it for you."

"Good of you, Mr. Draconian," he said. "I'm Tony Romagna, since introductions seem to be in order."

"What do you do, Tony?" I asked.

"I'm an investor."

"An investor of what, if I may ask?"

Tony laughed. "Kid, I like you and I guess you've made me all right. It doesn't matter. I have interests in Vegas, Miami and Atlantic City. I'm here in Paris for a little vacation. And also to look after the interests of a friend."

"What friend? Why are you following me? Or is it Rachel?"

"I like the way you just come out with it," Tony said. "You don't do any song and dance pretending you're not scared. Tell you what, I'm going to give you a little tip."

"I'm ready," I said, bracing myself for anything.

"The best Italian restaurant in this city is La Dolce Vita on the Avenue des Ternes. Tell 'em Tony Romagna sent you. Got it?"

I nodded, bemused. Tony winked and turned, almost losing his balance as he lurched against a trashcan. He nodded to me again and walked off. I watched him go, then decided it was time for a drink.

It was funny about Romagna. You get so used to the idea of fat men being light on their feet that you're a little thrown when you meet one who's as clumsy as you'd expect a fat man to be if the folk wisdom concerning these things hadn't led you astray. By clumsy, I don't mean that Romagna tended to tip over when he leaned too far to one side or anything dramatic like that. No, you could see at once that there was nothing haphazard in Romagna's clumsiness, nothing *clumsy.* There was skill in his careful ineptitude, an eerie intentionality. You could see it in his eyes, a dark glowing hazel, the attentive, inhuman eyes of a man who misses nothing, a man who does not possess the unselfconscious grace of the truly clumsy. There was calculation in Romagna's movements, and in his lurching gait I could sense a dark lucidity, made all the worse because it was a burlesque of itself. All this combined with his small chin and little rosebud mouth, which gave him a sinister rather than a weak look.

Romagna had the smooth rosy skin of a fat man, but beneath the show of health you could sense a cadaverous pallor, as though he were feigning health itself.

I saw now that Romagna was perhaps a better mime than Arne. He was doing an imitation of a New Jersey mafioso trying to hide his affiliation under a cloud of persiflage. Unless that were feigned, too.

Rachel found me some hours later in Harry's New York Bar near the Opéra. Harry's is dark polished woods and American voices and is the sort of place that tolerates quiet drunks, as long as they leave the other customers alone. I was a very quiet drunk. They probably thought I was crazy when I asked for saki, but the stuff works on me like a psychedelic, and I find it hard to worry when I have enough of it in me.

"You're drunk," Rachel said.

"Nobody's perfect," I told her.

"Did you find out anything about that guy who you say has been following you?"

"His name's Tony Romagna."

"Why is he following you?"

"Mr. Romagna didn't seem fit to enlighten me as to that. Mr. Romagna said that he was in Paris to enjoy a brief vacation and look after a friend's interests. Any of that mean anything to you?"

She shook her head. "It can't have anything to do with me."

"What about Alex?"

"How should I know? Did this Romagna say what he wanted?"

"Not a clue."

Rachel frowned, bit her lower lip gently, and said "What do we do now?"

"We go for dinner," I told her, "at La Dolce Vita on the Avenue des Ternes. Romagna said it was the best Italian food in Paris."

"Big deal," Rachel said. "I'm not in Paris to eat *spaghetti* for chrissakes."

"It's the only lead we've got," I said. "If it *is* a lead, which it just might be."

The food at Dolce Vita was quite good, as a matter of fact, though I'll spare you the menu this time, except to mention that the cannellonis were exceptional. It was a night for confidences. But no one came over to our red-checkered tablecloth, leaned over the candle guttering in the Chianti bottle and said, "I have a tale to tell." Not just then, anyhow. Nor did we have much to say to each other. Rachel seemed preoccupied, depressed. She seemed to have a hangnail on her left little finger, and she kept on biting at it.

We left around half past nine in the evening, by different cabs since we were going in different directions, Rachel to the Crillon in the Place de la Concorde, me to an evening in the cafés, and then back to the Cygne and to bed.

CLOVIS 15

IT WAS A bright, beautiful morning when I left the Hôtel du Cygne to go to the casting call at the old Gaumont Studios in upper Montmartre. I decided that I really should conserve some of Rachel's money, so instead of taking a taxi, I walked to the Châtelet Underground, then rode in a second-class car to Opéra, where I changed, then changed again at St-Lazare and finally got out at Lamarck Caulaincourt.

I caught glimpses of the beautiful basilica of the Sacré-Coeur as I walked down Caulaincourt to the entrance of the old Gaumont Studios, oldest in Europe, so I've heard.

From the outside the studio building resembled a cross between a fortress and a storage warehouse. The building was at the top of a steep hill. You left the shady plane trees of the boulevard and climbed up a series of steps to a steel mesh pedestrian bridge that crossed over to the Gaumont proper.

A receptionist took my name and told me where their casting call was being held. I walked down echoing corridors, past busy technicians doing esoteric things with tape reels. At last I came to the place where I was supposed to go.

Or at least I thought that was where I was supposed to go. I was on a huge sound stage. Low footlights illuminated the scene. The curtains had been pulled back, revealing a scattering of props: a mock-up of a cathedral door; a painted country meadow with river in background; a café set with real chairs and a zinc bar in the foreground.

As I crossed the stage, a spotlight came on from overhead and picked me up. It followed me as I crossed the stage, where it was joined by a second spotlight.

Somehow I felt challenged. I walked back to stage center and bowed. With the spotlights in my face I couldn't tell if anyone was out there. But I figured someone was listening.

"Messieurs et mesdames," I said, "thank you very much. It has been a pleasure to entertain you. What about a nice round of applause for the orchestra?"

From the darkened auditorium there came the sound of one person clapping. The houselights came up. There was only one man in the audience. He stood up and walked toward the stage, his steps slow, deliberate, theatrical.

When he got to the stage, I saw that he wore a dark blue blazer with a white pullover under it. He was perhaps in his forties, a tall man with a look of intense intelligence. I needed no introduction to know that this was the famous Gerard Clovis, enfant terrible of French cinema.

"Excellent," he said. "You are American? I congratulate you on your air of bewilderment, your projection of naïveté. I especially liked the way you stumbled over the power cable. Your face, too, has that homely innocence that identifies you as a fall guy. All in all, you are a perfect type, one who might have sprung full-blown from the forehead of the estimable Jim Thompson."

"Who?" I asked.

Clovis' lower lip curled in an indescribably derisive expression of scorn. "You do not even know the works of America's premiere writer of *policiers noir,* the famous Jim Thompson?"

I conceived an instant dislike for Clovis, along with a grudging admiration for his effrontery.

"No, I don't know any Jim Thompson," I told him. "I'm trying to trace a friend of mine who has gone missing. I was told that you had hired him for your movie."

"What is his name?"

"Alex Sinclair. An American."

Clovis' expression brightened. "Ah, of course, my newest discovery. He was quite perfect for the role. Do you bring me word of him?"

"I was hoping you knew where he was."

"He began working for me a few weeks ago. He didn't come to a costume call last week. He doesn't answer his telephone. And I begin shooting day after tomorrow. Frankly, I am in trouble over this."

"Sorry to hear it. I'll call you when I find out anything."

Clovis nodded in a vague sort of way. His mind was already far from Alex. He gave me a penetrating look. "Might I know your name?"

"I'm Hobart Draconian."

"Do you have any acting experience, Mr. Draconian?"

"No, I'm afraid not. Acting's not my line at all."

"Perfect," Clovis said, pronouncing it "parfay." "I despise the so-called professionals in this business. Big stupid faces and mincing diction. Antonin Artaud pointed the direction. I am the first to take it. Mr. Draconian, I would like to cast you in my movie."

"That's very kind of you," I said, "but it's out of the question."

"Never accuse me of being kind," Clovis said. "I have been called a pragmatist of the transcendental. And why is it out of the question? Do you have something more pressing over the next week or so than to participate in a film that is certain to make cinematic history?"

"Well, gee, I'd like to," I told him, "but I really have to find Alex. It's not only friendship, Mr. Clovis. It's a job."

Clovis mused. "Alex was very friendly with my camera crew. One of them might know something. And you should really talk to Yvette, the script girl."

"Great. How do I meet them?"

"That is a little difficult," Clovis said. "Everybody is scattered over Paris at present setting up my locations. But you will meet them all while you are working in my movie."

"Mr. Clovis, I admire your persistence, but I'm not going to be in your movie."

"But of course you are," Clovis said. "You seem to me a rational man. Working on my movie will give you access to all the latest Parisian gossip. You will meet several people who knew Alex well. I myself will assist you with your enquiries. And there is this to consider: perhaps some agent or producer will see your face when the movie is released, and will come to you with an offer of further work. This could be the beginning of a brilliant new career for you."

"I already have a career," I told him. "I'm an international investigator."

"Mmm, no doubt, but is it a *brilliant* career?"

I had to admit that, careerwise, the best was yet to come.

"Furthermore," Clovis said, "I pay in real money; francs you can spend right here in Paris, perhaps to improve your wardrobe."

That hurt. It's true that my Levis are a trifle tattered, and my blue workshirt has shrunk to where I can't button the sleeves, so I roll them back at the cuffs for that suave look of contrived nonchalance. And my Clarke desert boots have seen better days. Still, there was no reason to get insulting about it.

As for a career in the movies—that was the craziest idea I'd heard in a long time. It was so crazy, in fact, that I was more than a little amazed to hear myself say, "OK, you talked me into it. When do I start?"

"Day after tomorrow I begin shooting. I want you at dawn at Le Sélect, a bistro on the corner of the Boulevard Masséna and the Porte d'Italie. Seven sharp."

"OK, boss," I said, ironically, I hope.

THE ATTACK 16

I TOOK THE Métro back to Châtelet-les-Halles. There's a cinema on one of the lower levels which plays new and experimental films. I checked the program to see when they would be showing something by Clovis. In a week, I read, I would be able to catch a Clovis double bill: *Flesh, Desire and Squalor,* starring Simone Signoret, and *Orange Sunset,* with Alain Delon. I was keeping pretty good company in my new career.

I got on the escalator to return to the street level. That's when it happened.

This guy was riding the down escalator. Big, blond crew-cut type with tanned muscle and preternaturally white teeth. He was wearing surfing cutoffs, rubber flip-flops and a Hawaiian shirt, looking no more freaky than anyone else in the Forum des Halles, so I didn't give him another thought. That turned out to be a mistake.

Just as he came even with me he jumped across the border, or whatever-you-call-it between the up and down escalators, and came at me with his fists. He was muttering something, but I didn't register it at the time. I was too busy trying to figure out what to do.

As I have already mentioned, I am not one of your martial arts people. In fact, I do not believe in fighting. Therefore, if people insist upon thrusting a fight on me, I feel completely justified in utilizing unfair tactics.

As he came at me, I put out both hands to square him up, then kicked him clean in the crotch, or crutch, as the English say, the toe of my desert boot impacting nicely on the genital-laden inner thigh, just as old Lao Tse had taught me back in my student days at the Hokkaido Crotch-Kicking School.

Joe Dangerous collapsed head downward on the escalator steps, looking like something knackered. I received a nice round of applause from the crowd, but beat a hasty retreat because the next move after the Crotch Kick is the Full Speed Retreat, in case you've missed the sweet spot or encountered a steel cup. Retreat is always in good order after you kick a man in the crotch, unless you plan to go all the way and kill him, in which case you're well advised to do it there and then, before he has a chance to recover. Crotch-kicked men tend to be unbelievably violent.

It was a pleasure to come out onto the streets again. Suddenly it came upon me that I was in Paris. I had been so preoccupied with Alex that I had forgotten to take in the savoury immediacy of the nowness of my situation, drifting through the streets filled with amiable pleasure-seekers, some arm-in-arm, with the ubiquitous French policemen here and there, *les flics,* as we call them, walking in pairs, their short black capes billowing out behind them in the afternoon breeze. Cafés were on all sides of me, and the café is the ultimate civilized institution. People have tried to introduce them to the United States, but the results are mediocre. A blond college student who says, "Hi, I'm Harley," as he leads you to your table is not the same as the professional French waiter who comports himself with a dignity bordering on both sides of disdain.

No, the scene does not transplant. If you wanted to get the atmosphere just right in your Café de Paris in Heartland, U.S.A., you'd also have to import a couple of Moroccans in long robes to go from table to table selling souvenir drums. And you'd have to explain to the customers that nobody actually ever *buys* a souvenir drum, since these vendors are supplied by the Mairie de Paris to lend local color.

It is curious how we are always trying to obtain the virtues of There, the charming foreign place, for our uses Here, in the dull old hometown. Modern life consists of living Here and importing the important things from There: romance, fashions, lifestyles.

Here and There are eternal categories, never to be abolished or subsumed one under another. No matter how far you travel, you always live Here. And the place you're trying to get to, where the romance and adventure are, and the culture, is There, out of reach.

When you transport yourself physically from Here to There a curious condition ensues. First there's the illusion of having arrived There at last, where the good things are. You even get to enjoy a brief period during which time There retains its pristine quality, when things stand out in all their uniqueness; but the decay of strangeness is already taking place, perceptual fade-out, habituation, and soon what you behold is no longer charming, but merely quaint. All too soon, There turns into just one more Here.

One good thing that happens is that Here, after you absent yourself from it long enough, reverts to its There state. This is automatic, just like all Theres become Heres after you occupy them.

Here and There. You and It. Eternal categories, opposition, struggle. You versus It. The conquest of It by You. The eternal law by which strangeness is converted into familiarity.

I was musing on these and similar matters, as I strolled the sidewalks of the inner city which lies at the center of the City of Light. For mark my words, the area which I call Châtelet-les-Halles, between the Rue de Rivoli and the Rue Étienne-Marcel, and further bounded east and west by the Boulevard Sébastopol and the Rue du Temple, is a miniature hypermodern city where the ancient and the contemporary are thrown into constant abrupt juxtapositions. Interpenetrating in a small space of no more than several acres, you have a major modern art museum, a rail and subway terminus, a street of sex shops, a fountain filled with fire-swallowers and glass-eaters (tough-looking gentlemen accompanied by their girlfriends, who carry the lunch and the bottle of gasoline). Stone façades both ancient and modern connect on different levels. There are open spaces and closed spaces, all bound together by curving concrete walls and incorporating, here and there, an ancient structure. The South Americans have their own cafés in this quarter, places to meet in the ever-renewing exile that is the fate of modern South America. They come to Paris with their songs and their politics, and they are but the latest wave. Still here are all the other exiles, from the Maghreb and black Africa, from Iran and the Arab countries, from wherever dissidence is punished by long jail sentences or death.

Burdened with my thoughts, I ate dinner in one of the little restaurants on the Rue des Blancs and returned to my hotel room. I had been planning to freshen up and then go out again, to savor the Paris night and perhaps turn up a lead or two about Alex. Instead, I decided to lie down on the bed and indulge in melancholia. As I fumbled for the wall switch, a voice said from within my room, "Don't bother with the light just yet, *mon vieux.* It's much more comfortable here in the dark."

4

THE INTRUDER 17

ALTHOUGH THE VOICE hadn't said so, I assumed that its possessor was carrying a gun. I would have been, if positions had been reversed. So I decided to make no precipitate movement, nothing that would alarm the voice (though he'd sounded cool enough) into firing prematurely, or, shall we say, mistakenly. Nor, given my assumption, was there any efficacious action for me to take at the present moment. I had already closed the door behind me. There was nowhere to go.

"May I sit down?" I asked.

"Suit yourself," said the voice. He was speaking English, but with a French accent, as I might have expected. Moonlight streamed in through the tall, white-curtained windows, throwing a patch of yellow light on the floor and lending a ghostly illumination to the entire room. The armoire crouched in the corner like a fabulous beast. An armchair suggested itself out of the gloom, and I sat down in it.

After a suitable interval I said, "OK, are you going to tell me what this is all about or do we just sit around in the dark?"

"I'm acting on behalf of some friends," the voice said.

"Just what does that mean?" I enquired.

"It has come to our attention that you're looking for Alex Sinclair."

"That is correct," I said.

"Perhaps my friends could help."

"Sure. I pay for information. Tell your friends to give me a call. Early afternoon is a good time. Or leave me their number on your way out and I'll call them."

"I think it would be best if we went to see them now."

"I'd love to," I said, "but actually I've got a date in a few minutes. Why don't we set up a meeting? Lunch tomorrow sound good? I'm buying."

"Nice try, M'sieu 'Ob, but no go. My friends insist upon seeing you now. Are you going to come along nice and quiet, or are you going to give me trouble?"

"That depends," I said, "entirely upon whether or not you are armed."

"Make no mistake," he said. "I am armed."

"That's easy enough for you to say," I said. "But am I just supposed to take your word for it?"

"All right," the voice said. "Turn on ze light."

I complied. The overhead light revealed a man of middle years and sinister mien. His face was sallow and pocked. Blue stubble showed beneath his jaundiced skin like the bristles of a steel brush poking through an olive-drab bedsheet. He was wearing a long black overcoat and a black fedora. He looked like an intellectual dressed up as a thirties gangster; the sort of thing the French do so very well. In his right hand, a blued steel automatic winked wickedly.

"I'll assume it's loaded," I said. "There is such a thing as carrying credulity too far. Where are we going, and are you going to keep that pointed at me in the street?"

"It will be in my pocket," the guy said, pocketing the automatic. "Don't make me fire, thereby ruining two suits of clothes, to say nothing of your health."

And so out we went into the June night.

Paris is well known to be an exciting city, especially when you walk through it with a gun in your ribs. Thoughts of escape ran through my mind like small gray rabbits. What was to prevent me from suddenly breaking into a sprint, running up an alley, into a theater, or a bar, or a sex shop, or even ducking into the gendarmerie past which our footsteps were now leading us. Reluctantly, I put aside the idea. The black swans of caution brought me back to my senses: any sudden movement on my part could touch off this galoot's adrenalin-charged reflexes. If there were a hair trigger beneath his tensed trigger finger, a sudden move on my part might cause him to shoot me even before he had time to decide not to. And of course, he could probably get away with it since no one pays attention to noise in Paris unless it is loud enough to be a bomb or repetitive enough to be a machine gun.

And so I walked on. And as I walked, I thought. One of the advantages of taking an evening stroll with a gun in your ribs is the way it promotes a very real appreciation of even the most evanescent sensory pleasures, such as the sight of an old friend on the sidewalk, his face painted white, mimicking people.

"Hi, Arne," I said as we passed, hoping he'd read the note of desperation in my voice.

Arne made an exaggerated bow, stuck his hand into his right hand pocket in imitation of my abductor and fell into step beside and slightly behind us. What a time for him to play the fool! Arne's face took on an expression of worried evil. His eyes slunk back and forth. He did furtiveness to perfection, and my abductor didn't like it. He made a menacing gesture at Arne. Arne returned the gesture with exaggeration.

That was my chance. During the few moments that this byplay took, I managed to slip away.

Or rather, I *would* have managed to slip away if I hadn't noticed, in the crowd, the indisputable plum shape, dark blue suit and red carnation of Mr. Tony Romagna.

I decided that I was faced with too many mysteries and that I'd better solve at least one of them immediately.

"Put away that silly gun," I said to my abductor. "Lead me to wherever you're taking me."

"I am just supposed to trust you?"

"That's right."

He gave me an ironic look, but he did take his right hand from his pocket.

"You know," he said, "they told me you were a little different."

"I suppose I am," I said.

"What they didn't mention is that you are downright silly. My name is Etiènne. Come and meet the boys."

And so we marched onward into the night of terminal ironies and faint transparent ecstasies, the accordion-haunted night of Paris, our lady of the roasting chestnuts.

ETIÈNNE 18

Etiènne was a little nervous. It may have been his first abduction. But he was working hard to stay cool. "Come on," he said, "we'll take a cab. And don't try to kid around with me. I still 'ave ze gun."

A taxi stopped and we got in and Etiènne gave an address in the thirteenth arrondissement near the Porte d'Italie. No sooner were we underway than we heard something growling from the front seat, passenger side. Then we noticed the large black French police poodle sitting there. It was looking at us hard with its glittery attack dog eyes and making those scary sounds dogs make when they peel their lips back over their teeth and come on like King Kong having a seizure.

"What's the matter with ze dog?" Etiènne asked.

"It is, perhaps," the driver said, "that one of you gentlemen has a gun, n'est-çe pas?"

The dog meanwhile was working herself into an hysterical lather. Her fur stuck out like electrified fleece and yellow globules of what looked like corrosive sublimate ran down her fangs, while her eyes flashed green and red, the devil's stoplight.

Etiènne made a quick decision and said, "Yeah, I got a gun, so what?"

"It is indifferent to me," the driver said, shrugging, of course, "but the dog, she does not like it."

"Well, can't you speak to her or something? A man has a right to have a gun; it has nothing to do with ze dog; do you understand?"

"One is not dense, m'sieu," the cab driver said. "It deranges me to have to admit that while your reasoning is sound, your grasp of the essentials is imperfect. A dog cannot be reasoned with, and so, in her implicit stubbornness, she must be considered part of the given, implacable environment rather than a malleable player. To simplify matters, it would please the dog if you put your gun very carefully on the front seat. I will return it to you at the conclusion of the journey and everyone will be satisfied."

Etiènne didn't feel that *he* would be satisfied, but there wasn't a whole lot he could say about it, especially to a Parisian taxi driver with a police poodle riding shotgun for him.

Etiènne leaned past the dog's bristling wedge-shaped head, the blazing eyes never leaving his hand, and put the gun gently on the front seat. He sat back, but the dog continued to glare at him.

Etiènne endured it as long as he could, then said, "I did what you suggested; must she continue to stare that way?"

"Pay it no attention, m'sieu," the taxi driver said. "She means nothing by it; it is merely her way."

Etiènne stared straight ahead as we drove through the night-bright streets of the city of paradox, shaking his head slightly. I heard him mutter to himself, "Faked out by a dog. How about that?"

And then we were at the address he had indicated. Etiènne paid off the driver, retrieved his automatic, and we stood together on the pavement as the taxi drove away.

Etiènne watched it for quite a while even after it was out of sight. I waited for a while, then said, "So what happens now?"

Etiènne gave a start like a man awakened out of a dream, or perhaps into one, and said, "I don't know."

"What do you mean, you don't know?"

"I mean I can't remember ze address. Let's get a drink. I've got to pull myself together."

JEAN-CLAUDE 19

WE FOUND A bistro near Tolbiac. There I stood Etiènne to a cognac and I had an Orangina. Etiènne hadn't really forgotten where he was going. It was just the sort of statement that a man of his excitable though deeply repressed nature was apt to make.

I learned a little about him in the Gauloise-laden smoke of the bistro filled with laughter and accordians. He was a Corsican, but, unlike so many of his fellows, not tough. On the basis of his looks and the island's reputation, he was always being given jobs like this. It wasn't what he would have chosen, but then, which of us has much choice in these matters?

We walked a couple blocks on Masséna, then turned left onto the Avenue de Choisy for a few blocks, then stepped into the Chinatown that has sprung up around here. Sprawled beneath a group of high-rise buildings named after composers and painters—Puccini, Picasso, Rembrandt, Cézanne—were innumerable small shops and restaurants, where you can get Vietnamese, Laotian and Cambodian cuisine, most of it tasting like Chinese food would taste if you added fish oil to it. The little open-air markets in this vicinity were filled with oddly shaped vegetables and improbably colored fruits. The tall, modern buildings were filled with Boat People, so I've heard, resettled by the French for those who could claim French nationality from the old Indochina days. It's said that the police stay out of this district; the Indo-

Chinese (or whatever overall generic term they're called by) police themselves. Occasionally a body falls out of one of the upper levels, a defaulter on gambling debts usually. Skyscraper justice, they call it.

We cut through back streets to the Avenue d'Ivry, past a mixture of oriental eating places and Algerian couscous joints. Etiènne took me into an alley that led into a cobblestoned courtyard. Apartments opened on three sides of the courtyard. We crossed to one and Etiènne tapped on the door.

The door swung open. A figure stood there, backlighted in the doorway. Even in silhouette, and after ten years, I could recognize Jean-Claude.

"Have any trouble?" Jean-Claude asked Etiènne.

"Yeah, some," Etiènne said. "But it wasn't his fault."

"Come on in, 'Ob," Jean-Claude said. "We have some talking to do. I'm glad you didn't try to get away."

"You could have saved yourself the theatricals," I told him. "I was trying to find you, as a matter of fact."

"I'm sure you were, 'Ob," Jean-Claude said. "Come in and sit down."

We were in a sculptor's atelier. There were armatures of various kinds, buckets of clay, pieces of marble of various sizes. In neat racks on the wall were the tools a sculptor uses—mauls, chisels, those sorts of things. Jean-Claude gestured me to a seat. He sat down himself.

"Well, 'Ob," he said, a twisted smile on his narrow face, "it's been a long time."

Jean-Claude's suit was a blue and white pinstripe with sharp Italian lines rather than your natural-shoulder American look. His small, carefully trimmed black moustache might have tipped you off, too. It was quite unlike the big hairy macho soupstrainers that many Americans favor in emulation of their favorite pro football linebackers. Jean-Claude was unmacho in appearance, and yet you didn't feel he was a negligible man.

We talked for a while of old times and new. Jean-Claude had

just flown in from Cairo, where a deal involving small amounts of resinous substance had fallen through. Things weren't going too well for him. His life had fallen apart in Biarritz last month, when he had broken up with Suzie. He had walked out on her in a fit of pique, before he had taken the precaution of finding someone else to live with.

I noticed the small black ribbon in his boutonniere and enquired about it. It was for his Uncle Gasparé, who had been fished out of the Seine last week at the foot of the Pont Alexandre. Gasparé had been wearing a long, black overcoat with a mink collar. His hands had been tied in front of him and there had been a bullet hole in the back of his skull. Gangster slayings in Paris tend to have a certain panache.

Your French criminal is the most style-conscious in the world. Parisian underworld chic is modelled on the novels of Whit Burnett and James M. Cain. A lot of the clothing is copied direct from what Edward G. Robinson wore in his 1930s movies. Every self-respecting hood in Montmartre or Belleville dresses up; when you get to be a *capo mafioso,* or whatever its Corsican equivalent is, style becomes really important. Rumor was that Uncle Gasparé had been overstepping himself.

Jean-Claude was about five feet nine, weighing around a hundred and twenty pounds, had frizzy black hair and a hairline moustache. He was your typical French-Spanish-Italian sort of man, obviously nervous and high-strung, doubtless intelligent in an esoteric sort of way and filled with many little foibles incomprehensible to the straight-thinking citizens of North America excluding Mexico.

"'Ob," Jean-Claude said at last, "what in the hell are you doing back in Europe?"

"Why shouldn't I be back? I've got nothing to be ashamed of."

"You sold us out in Turkey, 'Ob. I've been waiting a long time to repay you for that."

"Like hell I did," I told him. "I saw Jarosik at the airport that day and I turned around and walked out. There was no way I could warn you or Nigel."

"The way I've heard it, you set us up. You sold us out to Jarosik and the Turks."

"That simply isn't true. When I got back to Paris, I did everything I could. I hired lawyers, arranged bribes—"

"Big deal," Jean-Claude said, twisting his lips into a characteristic sneer. "How much did the Turks pay you?"

"If I had done all that," I said, "why would I be here now? I didn't resist coming to see you. You can ask Etiènne."

Etiènne nodded in agreement. "We took a taxi here and there was zis dog—"

Jean-Claude silenced him with a gesture. "How the hell should I know why you're here now? Maybe you've gone even crazier than usual."

"I'm telling you, I did not turn you and Nigel in. I'm sitting here in front of you telling you that. If you don't believe me, there's not much I can do about it. Over to you, Jean-Claude."

He stared at me for a long time. At last he said, "Damn it, 'Ob, you're putting me into a terrible situation. Everybody knows you set us up. I'm supposed to take my revenge. You're trying to play on my sympathy, and it isn't going to work."

"That's what you think?" I asked.

"Yes, that's exactly what I think."

"Well, that's just great," I said. "So kill me, if that's what you're going to do, but please stop boring me to death."

He smiled faintly. "Same old 'Ob."

I also smiled faintly. I *was* the same old Hob. Crazier'n a bedbug. But rather more self-aware.

"What's this about you looking for Alex?" he asked.

"I need to find him for a client. I was trying to find you and Nigel. I want you to work for me on this case."

"Is that true, 'Ob? You really want us to work for you?"

"You know my way," I told him. "All my old friends are part of my organization. When you help me on a case, you get a cut of the action. Unless you kill me, of course. That changes everything."

"Is there really any money in this?" Jean-Claude asked.

I settled down for a nice little chat. Once they start talking money, you're safe from immediate peril.

5

CLOVIS 20

"AH, GOOD MORNING, Mr. Draconian," Gerard Clovis said. He was wearing gray twill riding jodhpurs, Frye boots and a yoke-back western shirt with mother-of-pearl buttons. This was his John Huston outfit, I later learned. He also had many other outfits, including a Federico Fellini outfit with floppy black hat.

It was just a quarter past seven. We were outside a large warehouse in the Kremlin-Bicêtre region of the thirteenth arrondissement, not far from where I'd been last night with Etiènne. There were two equipment trucks parked nearby, one crane-mounted camera, and a couple of handheld jobs. More lighting and equipment were inside the warehouse. There were quite a few people standing around, some technicians, some actors.

"Don't I get a copy of the script?" I asked.

"There is no script," Clovis said. He tapped his head. "It's all in here. The general plan. The broad conception."

"That's great for you," I told him. "But what are the actors supposed to do? Read your mind?"

"You will be told all you need to know," Clovis said. "I want you to have only a general idea. After that, just give me your interpretation, your reactions. I want you—all of you—to ad lib the scene, to be spontaneous. Don't worry about the dialogue; we're going to dub it in later, Italian-style."

He told me I was to enter the warehouse and go to the

second floor. I did so. The warehouse was a huge place, a man-made cavern above the ground. It was partially filled with sacks of vegetables, and stacked up along one wall were wooden skids with crates in orderly piles on them. The place smelled faintly of diesel oil and potatoes. There was office space on the second level. I went up there and shook hands with the camera crew. Then I was taken to a costuming booth in the back. Here I was introduced to Yvette, who looked me up and down and conferred with the wardrobe lady. After a brief discussion, they found an outfit for me: a white linen suit and panama hat, Tony Lama lizard-tip cowboy boots, brown checkered westernwear shirt with brown bandanna.

"Yvette," I said, "I understand that you know my friend Alex Sinclair?"

"Oui, m'sieu," she said, with that charming intonation that goes with a neat figure, black stockings and peasant skirts. She was a darling little thing, black haired and black eyed, with a natural friendliness that promised more than it was likely to deliver. But of course, you can never tell.

"When did you see Alex last?" I asked.

She looked thoughtful, another expression that she did well. "M'sieu 'Ob," she said in her delightful accent, "Alex asked me not to talk about his affairs. I must preserve his confidence, you understand."

"I do understand," I said, "and I approve. Alex told me the same thing himself. It's always been his way. Of course, he naturally breaks his rule for me. Especially as I am the bearer of good tidings."

"Ah, you talk too complicated for me," Yvette said, with a little laugh that was deliciousness itself. A fantasy formed up in my mind of living in an atelier with this delightful grisette on wine, love and remittance money.

"What I mean," I said, "is that I have money for Alex. Quite a lot of money. I'd like to give it to him."

Her expression brightened. "I can contact you, m'sieu, as soon as Alex calls me."

It was time to go Hollywood. I squinted at her and roughened my tone. "You don't understand, baby. Alex needs this money and I need some answers fast. Might be something in it for you, too, sweetheart."

She looked at me wide-eyed. I could see I was getting somewhere. And then a call came from outside, "M'sieu Draconian, we need you immediately!"

"I must think about zis," Yvette said, wide-eyed, full lips parted slightly to reveal tiny white teeth destined to nibble on my tenderer parts in the near future, or so I hoped.

" 'Ob! Where in hell are you!" This time it was Clovis himself calling, and he sounded annoyed.

I marched out to begin my acting career.

DANGER ON THE SET 21

A DISTANT, FAINT pounding of drums provided a staccato background as I stepped out into the corridor. Someone handed me a prop gun; this seemed to be some sort of *policier* I was acting in, though it was hard to be sure with a director like Clovis. After all, the gun could be a symbol, though I wasn't sure of what.

There was dry-ice smoke coming out from under the floorboards. Sequenced lighting along the corridor sent out pulses of orange and blue, not my favorite colors. Actually it was pretty neat, all things considered.

Behind me I could hear Clovis shouting, "Keep on walking; don't stop!" So I kept on. There were open doorways on either side of me, and one guy with a beret and a handheld camera was coming along behind me, panning each of the doorways. I panned them myself, with my eyes, of course, since nobody had given me a camera. Within each doorway was a scene or what they call a *tableau.* I saw people in frozen attitude staring at each other across suits of armor; Asiatics frozen in the attitude of gambling, mouths caught wide in the excitement; scenes of sexual explicitness veiled behind cheesecloth. And I thought of Jim Morrison singing, "Before I fall into the big sleep, I want you here . . . the scream of the butterfly. . . ."

And then I saw a face at the far end of the corridor, a woman's face, her hands beckoning to me. "Dialogue," Clovis hissed, and so I improvised:

"Hi, baby, you acting in this little number too? You wait right there for me, sweet thing; I'm a-coming down this here corridor as fast as I can, lickety-split."

Well, I mean it was just words to invent; they were going to dub the dialogue later, but I got caught up in it anyhow, so I didn't notice when the floor of the corridor came to an end. I couldn't have noticed it anyhow, since there was this smoke all over the floor up to my ankles.

You figure when professionals are shooting a movie, they have their act together, so I just stepped out and suddenly I wasn't standing on anything. I was falling.

DR. DADA 22

Paris is filled with places for every mood. I walked to the Avenue de Suffren, past the École Militaire, and then across the Champ de Mars toward the Eiffel Tower. I found a park bench and sat down.

The clarity and order of a French park promote logical thinking. Well-ordered greenery, dust motes in the afternoon sunshine, and little girls in white and gray school uniforms. You come to believe that God speaks French and is inclined toward irony.

Through my haze of abstraction, I slowly became aware of the old gentleman sitting on the bench beside me. It was a surprise, but not really a shock, for me to discover that he wore a black felt hat of antique shape over his powdered peruke. He had on a double-breasted fawn greatcoat with two rows of shiny buttons, silver or pewter. Another peek confirmed that he had green satin breeches that came to the knee, and below those were dove-gray silk stockings terminating in funny black shoes with square white metal buckles.

"Yes, take a good look, Hob," the old gentleman said. "And then dismiss me with one of your clever rationalizations."

A shudder passed through me. I knew that this was a time of testing, and it had come upon me before I was really prepared. I let my breath out slowly and turned to address him.

"Always pleased to meet an anomaly," I said. "I've been feeling a bit insubstantial myself of late. Do you have a name?"

"I have many names," he said in a teasing voice. "But I'll give you a clue or two. I'm known sometimes as Dr. Dada, and I'm a close friend of Siegfried Surreal. You've remarked yourself on the power that the Second Surrealist Manifesto still exercises over the minds of men. You suspect that the true nature of existence is difficult for an Anglo-Saxon to examine with the blunt instrument that is his mind. Common sense condemns you to a prosaic world, but you know it's the great enemy, and you came to France to find weapons to use in your grand struggle against reality. Confess it, Hob; you came here to talk with me."

"Yes, but who are you?"

"Among other things, I am that which eludes the web of your ratiocination."

He smiled at me, a smile of Voltairean subtlety. I felt myself on the verge of some vast breakthrough, some insight that would explain what I was doing here, some knowledge that would help me pull together the disparate strands of my life.

Then his image began to waver. I had a moment of vertigo, and was surprised to find myself, without apparent transition, lying on my back staring up at the sky. My head was resting on something soft: two rounded thighs beneath a long black cotton skirt.

" 'Ob! Are you all right?"

I looked up into Yvette's dark eyes. I was lying on my back on the ground floor of the warehouse. I remembered that I had been on one of the upper floors, walking down a corridor, when something had happened. Then I remembered: the floor had given way beneath me, and I had clutched at an electrical cable. It had broken my fall, but my weight had pulled me free of it and I had come down on the warehouse floor.

" 'Ob!" It was Clovis, bending over me. "Are you all right?"

I got to my feet cautiously, more than a little reluctant to leave the warm comfort of Yvette's lap. I took a few steps, flexed various muscles, discovered that I was bruised here and there but not broken.

"Thank God you are all right!" Clovis said. "I am having this accident investigated. I do not know how it could have happened. There was a hole in the corridor, Hob, and someone had put a piece of cardboard over it. It was inexcusable carelessness."

I could hear the familiar two-tone wail of a French police car. I wished that Clovis hadn't called the police. There was sure to be trouble when they learned that I was working on a film without a green card. It was even conceivable that I could be expelled from the country.

As it turned out, I needn't have worried. But of course, I couldn't have known I'd meet Inspector Fauchon.

EMILE FAUCHON 23

EMILE FAUCHON WAS a short, dumpy Inspector of Police with a droll Gallic eye and that liveliness of expression that is part of the great Gallic inheritance. He had coarse black hair cut in a short brush, large, lustrous brown eyes, sallow skin and a heavy stubble, recently shaved and powdered. His heavy eyebrows met above his nose, which was strong and slightly hooked. His lips were narrow, downturned. He arrived in a plain Peugeot, looked over the site of the accident, nodded and grunted as Clovis explained what had happened. He said little, made an occasional note in a small black notebook which he kept in a breast pocket of his dark three-piece suit. After he had looked everything over to his satisfaction, he turned to me.

"M'sieu Draconian, you have had a very close call. Are you entirely recovered now?"

"I'm fine," I told him.

"Then perhaps you would accompany me to the Sélect Café around the corner. We could have a cognac while I take your statement."

Le Sélect was a workingman's café, very popular in the *quartier.* White tile floor. Zinc bar. On the small, streaky television, a soccer game in progress, what the Europeans call football because they don't know any better. Or we don't.

It was late morning, and we were able to find a table in back without difficulty. I ordered a café au lait and a croissant, Fauchon a cognac and an espresso. The air was heavy with the smell of coffee, chicory, black tobacco, white wine and pernod. Fauchon questioned me, but more as one learning about an acquaintance than as a policeman talking to a suspect. I was a little uncertain about my right to conduct an investigative business in France, so I told him that I was an old friend of Alex Sinclair, which was true, and that I was looking for him, both out of my own interest and on behalf of a friend.

Fauchon made occasional notes, but mainly he just listened, his heavy-lidded eyes slit against the smoke from his Gauloise, resting his dark, closely shaven jowl against one chubby fist. He made a note of the spelling of Sinclair, and said he would look into it, and might perhaps have some information for me in a day or two.

We shook hands and Fauchon got back into his car, to return to the Préfecture, I suppose, that being what French police inspectors do when they are away from it. I returned to the warehouse and Clovis.

Clovis was directing the setting up of another scene in the warehouse. He seemed subdued, thoughtful.

"Thank God you are not hurt," he said. "This should never have happened. Fauchon will get to the bottom of it, however."

"The bottom of what? I thought it was an accident."

Clovis shook his head. "The only accidents on my sets are those I plan. This, I can assure you, was not planned by me. Come here, let me show you something."

I followed Clovis back to the upper level. We walked down the corridor to the place where I had fallen through. Clovis showed me how the floor supports, joists I suppose you'd call them, had been sawn through and then neatly fitted back into place. Loose rubbish had been strewn over them. It was as neat a deadfall as I've ever seen.

"But who did it?" I asked. "And why?"

"Interesting questions," Clovis said. "I'd hoped you might have some answers."

"Why me?"

"You're the person most apt to know who would like to see you dead."

"But I don't know."

"Then perhaps you should find out."

SECOND THOUGHTS 24

I HAVE NOTICED that private detectives do not spend much time discussing the injuries incurred in the line of duty, or whatever it is they call their work. They all seem to have this incredible ability to shake off serious beatings, sometimes with blunt objects, with a remark to the effect that they were a little stiff the next day but a good shower and massage would take care of it.

There is reason for this reticence, of course. Most private detectives tend to be heavily muscled mesomorphs, whose idea of a really good time is a workout in the local gym with their buddies around a Nautilus machine. I'm talking about the sort of person who plays handball when he's bored instead of lying down on a couch and waiting for the mood to pass like any normal human being. People like this have a lot to be stoical about.

I'm not like that. I bruise easily. The contusions I suffered from that fall in the warehouse in Bicêtre left ugly yellow and purple blotches. I'd probably have them for months. And they hurt. I won't mention it again, but I did want you to know.

I returned to my hotel room, had a long soak in the tub, and a couple hours' sleep. After that I felt almost well enough to keep my date that evening with Yvette.

Almost, but not quite. I just couldn't face the perfumed decadence of the Paris night, not even for Yvette. I was still thinking about that old guy in the funny hat I'd hallucinated earlier. And I was thinking about this whole case involving Rachel and Alex, thinking vague, discontented thoughts which I wouldn't care to reveal, but will anyhow. I was thinking that I was being pretty poorly paid for what was turning out to be a complicated and dangerous job. I was thinking that it was all getting to be a little much. I was approaching a dark moment; I could feel it; you always know when you're going into a tailspin. I wondered what in hell I was doing back in Europe. I began to relaize, with dismay, that I had done it again, sold myself a bill of goods, plunged myself into complications and risk because of some romantic fallacy concerning a Paris that never existed, and a me who never existed, either. I had tried to make a livelihood out of a romantic halo, the warm glow of temps perdu in which I wrap my memories, building a kingdom of nostalgia and hot air. As if my years in Europe hadn't been bad enough, here I was trying to do the whole thing again.

Have you ever noticed that anyone can have a crisis in a detective novel except the detective himself? Well, just remember that you saw it here first—a detective turning resolutely away from his appointment with a prime informant. Instead, I went downstairs and asked the concierge if she could send a telegram for me. She could. I wrote, DEAR RACHEL, I QUIT. LOVE, HOB. and had it sent to the Crillon.

You could say I was overreacting. But the fact is, I hate being dropped through floors. Especially when I'm not even making a profit on the case.

RACHEL AGAIN 25

TWO HOURS LATER I was taking a nap, when Rachel came to the door. "What do you mean, you quiet?" she asked.

"Let me see that," I said, taking the piece of paper out of her hand. It was my telegram. "I said 'I quit,' not 'I quiet,' " I told her. "The bloody frogs get everything wrong."

"Not so high on Europe today, are you?"

"My enthusiasm began to fade at the precise moment I fell through the floor at Kremlin-Bicêtre."

"Well, you shouldn't have been acting in a movie anyway. I hired you to find Alex, not start a new career."

"On the money you're paying me, I need another job in order to support myself while I'm working for you. You know the motto of my guild: Don't risk your life for *bupkes.*"

"I don't know that word," Rachel said, "but I guess I understand what you're saying. I want you to continue. What do you want?"

"First, a little honesty."

"Are you accusing me of lying?" Rachel asked. Her voice, as you might imagine, was cold.

"No, not at all," I said. "I just want you to tell me the truth."

"You're contradicting yourself," Rachel said. A little less coldly. "What do you want to know?"

"Why do you want to find Alex?"

"But I've told you," she said. "He's a friend. He's missing. I care about him."

"Go on," I said.

"Go on where?"

"What's the payoff?"

"I honestly don't know what you're talking about."

"Rachel," I said, "I like you. But if what you've just told me is the truth, the whole truth, nothing but the truth, then we'd better call it quits. I should be back in the States for my daughter's graduation anyway."

"But why are you suddenly going to quit like this?"

"Because, Rachel, this thing is getting dangerous. Lots of people seem to be involved, and there seems to be something, or maybe several somethings, that I know not of. That puts me at a disadvantage, since everyone else knows more than I do. What I do know is this." I paused dramatically.

"What?" she asked.

"I know that Alex hasn't simply dropped out to go run with the bulls in Pamplona. I know he's involved in something complicated and probably illegal. And I've got a feeling that a lot of money is involved."

"What makes you think so?"

"A lot of people are interested in Alex. People don't keep up that kind of interest unless there's money in it."

She thought about that. "I see what you mean," she said after a while.

"Good. Then what are you going to tell me?"

"Hob," she said, "the best thing I can say at this point is, it's worth five thousand dollars to me to find Alex."

"Is that real money or play money?"

She flushed. "Are you calling me a liar again?"

"Not at all. I'm just pointing out that I have expenses, people to hire, bribes to spread around, plus my own payroll to meet."

"I can give you a thousand dollars right now." She opened her purse, looking at me.

"Tell you what," I said, "give me two thousand now, and eight more when I turn him up."

"That's ten thousand dollars!"

"Yes."

"This isn't a very nice thing you're doing, holding me up like this in the middle of a case."

"You can take your complaint to the guild. It's little enough, considering that you still haven't told me anything useful."

"All right," she said. "How soon do you think you can turn him up?"

"Get your money ready," I said. "I figure three days, a week at the most, and this case is going to blow wide open."

Afterwards I was to marvel at my prophetic soul.

6

HARRY, MARIA 26

Harry Hamm felt a little self-conscious, walking down the pier at the port of Ibiza with Maria Guasch beside him. But he felt good. Maria was a handsome woman with a lot of class, and he was happy to be with her. He had begun hoping that they wouldn't find out about the Guasch brothers too soon, so maybe they could have lunch together.

But then Antonio Plannells told Maria that he'd seen the brothers leave. Once beyond the breakwater they'd set a course for Barcelona.

Maria frowned when she heard that. Barcelona was far from their usual fishing grounds. "Why would they be going there? Antonio, could you try to call them on your radio?"

"They'd be beyond my range," Plannells said. But he agreed to give it a try. He told Maria and Hamm to wait on the deck while he went below into the crowded, messy little cabin and tried to raise the brothers on short wave.

It was a bright, fair day. The wind whipped the little dark tendrils of hair that escaped from Maria's kerchief. A white cruise ship from Mallorca was just coming around the island of Tagomago. Harry found that he was ridiculously happy, and for no reason he could think of.

Then Plannells came back. "I didn't get them. But I talked to Diego Tur, who saw them before he turned for home."

"Where were they?" Maria asked.

"About twenty miles east of Cadaqués."

"Where's that?" Harry asked.

"North of Barcelona," Maria told him, "almost in the Golfe du Lion."

She turned to Antonio Plannells and questioned him in rapid-fire Ibicenco. Then turned back to Harry.

"They seemed to be going north. In the direction of Montpellier, or Marseilles."

Harry drove Maria to her finca. He wanted to ask her out again but he didn't know how to go about it. You just didn't invite Ibicenca women out for a drink.

Later that day, reading the newspaper in a café in Santa Gertrudis, he came across an article, on page five of the *International Herald-Tribune.* Harry read it twice, then decided he'd better telephone Hob.

Making an international telephone call from Ibiza is a major undertaking that can use up the better part of a day. Harry drove to Santa Eulalia, Ibiza's third largest town. Some sort of festival was going on; the streets were crowded and there wasn't a parking space to be found. Harry circled the streets twice, finally drove nearly a quarter of a mile out of town to the Hotel Ses Rocques where his friend Carlitos, who guarded the parking lot, let him park free. Harry started along the path back to town, exchanging good-natured pleasantries with friends and acquaintances he met along the way. He wasn't hurrying, because it wouldn't do to hurry in Ibiza where time is measured by weeks and months rather than minutes and hours. But he was feeling a little edgy because he did have a message to deliver, and the indolent charm of Ibiza stood in his way of getting the job done.

Harry came to the filled-up parking lot on the edge of town, walked through it, cut between buildings and reached the central promenade, the Calle del Kiosko. It was called this because at its upper end was an outdoor café where you sat and met your friends, or your enemies, or just plain anybody, Ibiza being that sort of place.

Harry had no time for pleasantries right then, although he had to engage in them, because no emergency was so great in Ibiza, not even your house burning down, that you would ignore the pleasantries. He nodded to the señora who did his shirts; he exchanged greetings with Irish Alec who ran El Caballo Negro, the bar where he mostly hung out. And at last he reached the telephone kiosko.

The telephone kiosko was the most recent sign of modernization in Santa Eulalia. Until a few years ago there was no public telephone in Ibiza. You had to get permission at one of the bars or restaurants or hotels if you wanted to make a call. But then La Compañía Telefónico de España put in a telephone exchange, a prefab cubicle about the size of a small trailer. Six telephone booths take up two walls. On your left as you enter is the desk where you place your calls. On the other side, a wooden bench where you can wait.

Don't bother taking out your telephone card. These phones don't even have a slot you can put it into. Here long distance calls are made the old-fashioned way, by having your operator talk to another operator and then seeing if between them they can locate your party.

In summer, in peak calling hours, this could become high comedy. The international telephone exchange was Santa Eulalia's introduction to high stress and modern living. There were people in it all day long, mostly foreigners, clamoring at José in the incomprehensible syllables of their unknown tongues. José, short, barrel chested, broad faced, a cheerful yet serious man, was not at all intimidated by the situation. Like many Spaniards, he loved an emergency and was able to take control instantly and get the job done. There was only one proviso: you shouldn't question his way of doing things, and above all don't tell him it's taking too long.

José coped, solving each problem as it came along. He spoke no language other than Spanish, but that has never stopped a Spaniard from making himself understood. One way or another, all the calls went through. From time to time José sent his little son Joselito out to get him an ice cream cone. It was hot work, placing international phone calls from Santa Eulalia in June.

Harry and José were friends. Harry spoke a crude Spanish set entirely in the present tense and employing the infinitive exclusively. He was understood by everyone.

Harry didn't mention that his call was urgent. He had been in Spain long enough to know that that attitude gets you nowhere. Tell a Spaniard that something is urgent and his mind goes on vacation. Urgent? Has someone been killed? That is the Spaniard's idea of urgent.

"Paris," José said, looking at the number Harry had written down. "Must be important, no?"

Harry shrugged his shoulders to show that this call was really a matter of no concern to him, so unimportant that he could scarcely understand why he had bothered getting out of bed to make it. Then he reflected; yes, maybe it did have some slight importance. He said, grudgingly, *"Bastante."*

Bastante means "enough," or "sufficiently." It is a seemingly inexpressive little word that can mean a great deal in the right corner of the Spanish-speaking world. Harry had learned that it was a word more decisive than the *urgencias* and *rápidos* of the Spanish language. Harry had learned that when José said something was *muy caro* it meant it was less expensive than something that was *bastante caro.*

"I'll get it for you right away," José said, disconnecting a lady who had talked long enough to her husband in Copenhagen. He put his hand on the handcrank—yes, you cranked these telephones like old U.S. Army field units—muttered, "Pues, a ver," and cranked.

And he got Paris just like that; sometimes it's like magic. And there it was: Harry was through; now if only Hob was on the other end.

ME, HARRY HAMM 27

I WAS JUST resting up in bed after a hard day of being pushed around by Jean-Claude and friends when suddenly there was Harry Hamm on the telephone.

"Harry? How are you!"

"Hot and tired, Hob, but bearing up. Got some news for you."

I had been so wrapped up in the concerns of the moment that I'd clean forgotten that my life did not consist of merely a single case, as seems to happen with so many private detectives in literature, who apparently live in a state of limbo between cases, with nothing better to do than indulge their alcoholic pursuits and eat at heartbreak diners full of cheap food and wisecracks. Real detectives, such as myself, have more than one case going at a time.

"Yeah," I said, "give it to me."

"Near as I can make out," Harry said, "those sailboards of yours are on a fishing boat bound for France." Harry told me that Industrias Marisol was run by Enrique and Vico. Enrique had gone to San Sebastián, and Vico had left the island by fishing boat. The boat seemed to be going to France. Harry presumed that Vico and the missing sailboards were aboard.

"I don't suppose you know where in France?" I asked him.

"I don't know for sure," Harry said. "These fishing boats

don't file flight plans. But I saw this article today in the *International Herald-Tribune.* Page five, lower right hand corner. It seems there's a sailboat race to be held tomorrow in the Honfleur harbor in France. What do you want to bet those boards end up there?"

"I think you've got something," I said. "Good going, Harry! So you'll fly into Honfleur and check it out."

"Hob," Harry said, "I can't leave Spain."

"Are you wanted for something in France?"

"Nothing like that. It's just that I've applied for my *permanencia.*"

"Merde," I said, in my anger slurring the italics. The *permanencia* is your permission to live permanently in Spain. It carries several privileges and a few obligations. To get it, you must fill out your forms, surrender your passport, and reside in Spain for six months. After that your passport is returned and you can come and go more or less as you please.

"When's your *permanencia* supposed to come through?"

"In about six weeks."

"This is damned inconvenient," I said. "Can't you get your buddy Belasco to get your passport back for you?"

"No sweat, if it were on the island," Harry said. "But you know as well as I do, all paperwork goes to Madrid."

I nodded, grinding my teeth. Bloody overcentralized Spain. I'm a regional autonomy man, myself.

"All right," I said. "I'll check it out myself."

HONFLEUR 28

I WENT TO the Gare Montparnasse and caught a train to Honfleur.

Honfleur is a couple of hours from Paris. It's an old port in Brittany on the English Channel. It played an important role during the Napoleonic wars.

I took a room at the Hôtel Arènes with a nice view of the harbor. I felt better immediately. From my window I could look out on the narrow cobblestoned streets, the steep church steeples, the cobblestoned ramp down to the harbor. I had noticed a few WELCOME SAILBOARDERS signs on the streets. Aside from that, there didn't seem to be much local interest.

There wasn't much to do in Honfleur, but that was all right by me. I strolled in the town and along the harbor, admiring the skies, which looked like the skies in French seascape paintings; I stopped at cafés here and there for coffees and apéritifs. I loafed and invited my soul.

When I returned to my hotel I wasn't entirely surprised to learn from the bell captain that a gentleman had asked for me, and was now awaiting my return in the lounge.

Looking into the bar, I saw the burly, familiar, tweed-clad back and leonine head of Major Nigel Wheaton.

I slid onto a stool beside him. "Hi, Nigel," I said.

As I have mentioned, I am not of the muscular persuasion. When there is anything dirty to do, I subcontract it. Why do it yourself when an expert is close at hand forever in need of money?

Nigel Wheaton was ex-Red Berets, a former colonel in Moise Tshombe's ill-fated army. Before that, he had lent a hand in various unpleasantnesses in Malaysia, Kenya, Brunei and Afghanistan. Wheaton was tall, and, when he forgot to hold in his stomach, portly. He had a full head of untamed reddish-brown curls, a curly beard and moustache. He looked a little like a lion, and a little like a Monty Woolley who had been left out in the sun too long. Nigel's face was a monument to tropical sunlight and hard booze. He was a complicated man with several different aspects. One of his best acts was the slightly stuffy British ex-army type. Comical, that one. He had other personas, too, and no one, not even Nigel, knew which was the real Wheaton.

"Jean-Claude said you had a job for us," Nigel said.

"How'd you know to look for me here?"

"I remembered you used to come here often in the old days, when you were fed up with Paris but not quite ready to return to Ibiza."

"You know my ways, Watson," I said.

Nigel nodded. "How's Kate, by the way?"

"Just fine," I said.

"Does she ever ask after me?"

"Not really, Nigel. Kate has put the good old days far behind her."

"Lovely woman, Kate," Nigel said. "Are the children all right?"

"Yes, fine. They didn't ask after you, either."

"Well, so much for the good old days. What's happening currently, Hob?"

"Alex Sinclair. Remember him?"

"Only too well," Nigel said. "For a while he had a finca adjoining mine in Ibiza. Devious Alex, the golden-haired boy. I was best man at his second wedding, you may remember. I can't remember now if that was his marriage to Margaret or Catherine."

"What else do you remember about him?"

"He did a scam with Raúl Fauning, the art forger. Then worked for Bernie Cornfeld for a while selling imaginary real estate. Then returned to the States. Gave up his days of wild and illicit freedom and went to work for some big law firm in Washington, D.C. The last I heard he was living high on the hog in Georgetown."

"That's about the limit of my knowledge, too. I've been hired to find him. Seems he came to Paris about a month ago and disappeared."

"Who's hiring you? If I'm not being indiscreet by asking."

"No, you're on the payroll now, such as it is. The lady in question is named Rachel Starr, or at least that's the name she gave me."

"Never heard of her," Nigel said. "Not one of the old bunch, I presume?"

I shook my head. "I introduced her to Rus and he didn't know her. If Rus didn't know her, she wasn't on the scene."

"Why does she want to find Alex?"

"She won't tell me. It seems to be a personal matter."

Nigel smiled. "With Alex it usually is. What do you want me and Jean-Claude to do?"

"That should be obvious. Try to find something out. Specifically, what Alex was really up to, how and why he's disappeared, where he is now."

"Seems reasonable enough," Nigel said. "When are you coming back to Paris?"

"Soon," I said, unhelpfully.

"What are you doing here?"

"Another case," I told him.

"Well, old boy," Nigel said, "we're partners now. Fill me in."

So I told him about Frankie and what Harry had uncovered.

"You're going to intercept the guy here?" Nigel asked.

"Yes, assuming he and the sailboards do indeed come here. Maybe this whole thing can be settled easily."

"A lot easier than trying to establish jurisdiction, eh?" Nigel said. "Well, I suppose you know what you're doing."

I nodded; although I didn't, not really.

"Could you advance me and Jean-Claude a little something?" Nigel asked. "I believe you Americans refer to it as walking-around money."

I gave Nigel five thousand francs to split with Jean-Claude. I gave him a list of the people I had interviewed so far. He gave me a telephone number where a message could be left for him or for Jean-Claude.

"Are you taking the train back?" I asked.

Nigel shook his head. "I've still got the old Hispano-Suiza. See you in Paris."

He turned to go. I said, "By the way, Nigel . . ."

He turned, a splendid military figure with a slight paunch. "Yes, Hob?"

"About Turkey. I did *not* set up you and Jean-Claude."

"I know that," Nigel said.

"Jean-Claude didn't seem to believe me. How come you know I'm telling the truth?"

"I worked it out long ago. If I really thought you'd turned us in, Hob, we wouldn't be having this conversation."

"Why not?"

"Because you'd be lying at the bottom of St-Martin canal with my exercise weights tied to your ankles. See you in Paris, Hob."

MEETING VICO 29

THAT EVENING I took a taxi out to Honfleur's little aerodrome, which also served Le Havre and the Pays-de-Caux. It was a mild evening. To the east, a gray haze was visible over the Paris basin. The evening flight from Antibes was twenty minutes late. I was close to the passenger gate when they got off. There were many people on the flight. Only a few of them were men in the right age group. The rest were women, children, priests and military. There were also several South Americans, evident at once because of their serapes and tap shoes.

It was pretty easy to find an observation point where I could watch without being spotted. The coffee bar opposite the passenger gate had a large mirror in which I could watch the arrivals.

There were two priests, and a bunch of schoolgirls in school sweaters, maybe a volleyball team, the Nice High School All-Stars versus the Camargue Ducks. Maybe not.

And then I spotted the man. He came out of the aircraft and looked around, like he'd just come to the promised land. I saw the package come through. Five brightly colored sailbags, other colored canvas bags holding gear.

They came around on the baggage carrousel, and he took them off and stacked them neatly. A porter came over, took the bags out, gave them to a limousine marked Hôtel Ritz, Honfleur. Vico was about to get into the limousine when there came an announcement for him, a telephone call. He went to get it. When he got back, the limousine had left.

"Excuse me," I said. "May I offer you a lift into town?"

"I don't believe we've met," he said. "But I'd be very pleased. My luggage went without me."

He got in. I drove off.

"We haven't met," I told him, "but we do have a mutual acquaintance. We both know Frankie Falcone."

He stared at me wide-eyed. "Who did you say?"

I repeated it for him. "Frankie Falcone. I'm Hob Draconian, his manager and friend. I'm also a private investigator."

"So you know Mr. Falcone?" he said.

Vico was short, barrel chested, in his mid-twenties. He had dark, brutal good looks. But there was something wrong with them. Something ran across his face like a fissure in a cliff, some weakness not even buried under the surface, an exterior flaw to mirror an inner compunction. And it was impossible to think any thing of this face except for the drama it represented. What drama? Weakness versus strength, custom versus spontaneity, the reality principle versus the life of fantasy. I thought, there are so many of these short, dark, barrel-chested people, and for a moment he was as alien to me as a Javanese, or one of the inhabitants of Barsoom.

After giving me a long look, whose intent I did not find clear, Vico said, "You come to me from the great Mr. Falcone? America's premier maker of sailboards?"

"That is correct."

"But please, this is wonderful, let me buy you a drink! Next to meeting Mr. Falcone himself, this is the greatest pleasure I could imagine. Mr. Draconian, you have no idea what Falcone's sailboards have meant to me. Come into the bar, I must buy you a drink this instant, and we will talk."

People are sometimes hard to get close to in my line of work. They clam up, won't say a thing. But sometimes you get a break. Especially if you're me. I'm a private investigator who tends not to terrorize the people I interview. Quite the opposite. Malefactors have told me that, in my presence, they felt a burst of divinely inspired inner power, as though they could succeed forever in a world composed of types like me. In gratitude and grandiosity, they sometimes spill the beans.

But then sometimes you meet a type like Vico. Falling all over himself to talk to me. I followed him into the bar. Already I was getting an uneasy feeling. It's the feeling you get when they're not cooperative enough. Or when they're too cooperative.

Vico ordered champagne cocktails for us both. Fixing me with his beady black eyes, he said, "You cannot know how things were for me last year. My wife, Maria, had just lost her mind. She was suffering from the delusion that I was a vampire bat. Wouldn't let me anywhere near her. You can imagine the frustration on my part. I also had an argument with Enrique, my elder brother, who was also my partner in the scuba rental business we were then engaged in. This was before I knew anything of sailboarding. All I dealt with was the same dreary old stuff, scuba gear for brawny Germans or Frenchmen so they could go down to the depths of our beloved island, Ibiza, and take away the last of her rapidly dwindling underseas life on the ends of their spears. Scuba divers are a sinister lot, if you ask me, and it was irony that our business catered mainly to them. I won't bore you with the details of how I got into that unsavory business, except to say that it was the result of a curious bequest on the part of my Uncle Lluit, and is a story which has taken its place in the folklore of the island.

"So never mind how I got it, there I am in this detested business, and then one day I hear about sailboards. They had been around for quite a while, in fact, but when you are sunk deep in the sort of gloom that can come to a man only in a Catholic country with strong family ties when nothing is working out, you stop really tracking. A lot of important stuff was passing me by. For a five-year period I can't remember a single band name, nor the title of a movie. It is the dreaded cafard, some say caused or at least impelled by the southern wind, the sirocco or levanter, or khamsim as they call it in Israel, the wind of ill repute which visits our shores from time to time, a hot, dusty, dark wind of grit and irritability blowing out of Africa, bringing with it the dreaded mumbo jumbo and foreknowledge of bad times coming. That's how it was with me, and so the sailboard sensation hit me, belatedly, but with purity. I saw at once how these small boats, so easy to outfit, so simple to man, could become a pathway to ineffable regions, and lead one to areas of accomplishment of both an inner and an outer nature.

"I introduced sailboards into my store, trying now this design, now that, until I came at last upon the incomparable boards of the peerless Frankie Falcone of Hood River, Oregon. Up to this time I had been a merely competent sailboarder, one capable of beating up a windward leg, or whatever it was, with the rest of the pack, but never finishing first. But that changed when I tried my first Falcone board. I began to place in the winning numbers.

"I tried a second Falcone board. My success was even greater. I suddenly saw what I could do: obtain the necessary four or five boards and equipment and enter international competition. With just a few wins I could free myself of my brother Enrique's callous laughter, the jealous jeers of my father, the catcalls of my own generation who knew the names of the pop idols, but had forgotten their own souls. I could rise above all that, supported by victory money, and all I had to have was Falcone boards under my feet.

"The next step was inevitable. I hadn't told anyone of my intentions.

"It was expensive but I had to have the boards. It was the biggest gamble of my life, but I sent for them. When they arrived I summoned up all my courage and left the island, left my wife, brother, parents, just me and the boards and a change of underwear. And so I entered my new life.

"Another drink, Señor 'Obart! Let us signal the beginning of new life, away from all the sorrows and defeats of the past."

So said Vico and leaned back, beaming but sweaty, a man who felt better for confession, a man trembling on the threshold of transformation and a new life. I sympathized. So you can imagine what sort of a bastard I felt like, when, in the tones of flat pragmatism that I detest but live by all the same, I said, "That's all very well, Mr. Vico, and I do wish you a lot of luck in your new life. But how about paying for the boards, huh?"

The moment of retribution, the calling-forth of the reckoning! It is the private detective who brings forth this moment.

VICO 30

VICO SAID, "I beg your pardon?"

"The money for the sailboards. The money for Sr. Falcone."

"Ah, the money! Yes, I pay it!"

"You paid it? When?"

"Excuse me, I don't mean I already *did* pay it. I mean that I *intended* to pay it. Excuse me, my English not so good."

I let that go. "Can you pay it now, Mr. Vico?"

"Well, of course. That is, I suppose I can. But it may take a little while. A matter of days. Then of course I am going to pay."

"Vico," I said, "I'm not a cop, and even if I were, I couldn't arrest you in this country. There's no case against you in France. But we have our ways of getting deadbeats like you to pay up or wish you had. Have you heard of the newspaper treatment?"

"No, what is that?"

"We take out ads for a couple of weeks in your local newspaper, alluding to your debt and asking you when you are going to pay up. If this fails, we assess how much damage you caused our client and then we make that much trouble for you."

"In my case," Vico said, "that will be unnecessary. I have the money right here." Vico took out his billfold and removed a check. He showed it to me.

I looked. I saw a check drawn on the Banco de Bilbao for two million pesetas and change. It was made out to Frankie Falcone.

e check," I told him. "Why don't you give it to r
and we're square."

y I could!" Vico said. "But at present I have no money in this .. count. But I will have in a few days. I'll give it to you to give to your client this weekend, and time payment after Saturday."

"Why must we wait until then?"

Vico's eyes glowed. "Because Saturday is the day of the sailboard main event race in Honfleur harbor. Cash prizes. For first place, it comes to nearly twenty thousand dollars. I can win it, Sr. Hobart. I've already taken two first in Majorca, and one in Barcelona. I know that's not the big time, but it's good. I know who's racing here. I can beat them."

"I don't know," I said. "It's all pretty iffy."

"Of course it's iffy," Vico said. "I am a man who lives by translating fantasies into realities. The rise of any poor boy to top matador or jockey or sailboarder is beset by impossibilities."

I had no answer for that. Far be it from me to claim that the unlikely never happens.

"And think of the publicity for Falcone boards," Vico said. "When I win, it'll put Falcone boards on the world sailboarding map. Mr. Falcone will have to hire a factory to keep up with orders. How can you pass up such a chance?"

How indeed? And in fact, what other chance was there? I might be able to find a local lawyer and institute proceedings against Vico. But where would that get me? By the time the law had it sorted out, Vico and the boards would be long gone.

"Saturday," I said, "I will be in Paris."

"Then it will be my pleasure to come see you."

So I wrote out the name of my hotel for him. It really was time I got back.

HONFLEUR, ROMAGNA 31

My next caller was not long in arriving. It was evening, a few hours after Nigel's departure. The Palma–Orly flight had been delayed. I had finished *le grand plateâu des fruites de mer*—also known as the seafood dinner—at the hotel, and strolled down to the harbor for my evening constitutional. I wasn't entirely surprised when someone waved to me from a sidewalk café table, and called out, in the unmistakable accents of New Jersey, mother of corruption, "Hey, Hob! Come over and have a drink."

It was Tony Romagna. He had doffed his dark blue mafia suit and was now wearing a beige lounge suit with red piping along the lapels, the sort of thing they sell in the Short Hills Travel Boutique for affluent tourists in New Jersey. In it, Romagna looked like a beige whale with red piping on his fins.

"Hi, Tony," I said, sitting down at his table. "What brings you to this neck of the woods?"

"I heard this was a historical town," he said, smiling easy.

"You've picked a good place," I told him. "Did you know that Honfleur dates from the eleventh century? I'd especially recommend the church of Sainte-Catherine, and the shrine of Notre-Dame-de-Grâce."

"That sounds pretty nice," Romagna said. "Actually, I was hoping to run into you here."

"How'd you know where to find me?"

"You're not so hard to find, Hob," Romagna said. "Creature of habit, aren't you?"

"When I choose to be," I said, giving him a subtle look. "What do you want, Romagna?"

Romagna's broad face took on a serious look. He knocked over a wine glass, reinforcing his image of clumsiness, and said, "You're looking for Alex Sinclair." It was a statement rather than a question.

"I'm not admitting anything," I told him. "But what if I am? What's it to you?"

"I'm looking for Alex, too," Romagna said.

"Somehow, Mr. Romagna, that doesn't surprise me as much as you might think. Quite a few people seem to be getting interested in Alex."

"Do you know yet where he is?"

"I wouldn't be sitting in Honfleur if I knew that. And you wouldn't either."

"But you do expect to find him?"

I nodded. "The Alternative Detective Agency always gets its man."

"How would you like to work for me?"

"I don't know," I said. "What do you pay? Do you offer Major Medical? Is there a pension plan? What do you want me to do?"

"Obviously, I want you to find Alex."

"I'm already doing that."

"Yes, but for a different client. When you find him I want you to tell me first. I could run him down myself, of course—I've got plenty of connections in this town—but why should we duplicate our efforts?"

"That wouldn't be fair to my present employer," I said.

"Maybe not. But it would pay you well. And save you a lot of trouble."

"How well and what trouble?"

"I'll give you a flat five thousand dollars if and when you tell me where to find Alex."

"I like nice round numbers like that," I said. "Now tell me about the trouble."

Romagna smiled. For a moment he looked like a beat-up Rubens angel with blue jowls. "No trouble at all, if you play along."

"Mr. Romagna, I really need to know more than you're telling me. Who are you; whom do you represent; why are you interested in finding Alex?"

Romagna lurched to his feet, put down a handful of bills on the table more or less at random, straightened his whale suit.

"Five thousand dollars if you cooperate," he reminded me, as if I needed reminding. "Unending *tsouris* if you don't. You can get in touch with me at the Ritz. Do yourself a favor. Don't get dead." He strolled off.

I watched him cross the square and get into a chauffeured Peugeot 404. I watched him drive away. I noted down the license plate number, though I had no idea what to do with it. Then I finished the rest of my coffee. When the waiter came by, I paid for the drinks out of Romagna's bills, left a suitable tip, and pocketed the rest. Waste not; want not.

RETURN TO PARIS; JUANITO 32

I CAUGHT THE morning train back to Paris the next day, well satisfied with how things were going. Perhaps I hadn't made much progress on finding Alex or getting Frankie reimbursed for his sailboards; but at least the projects looked like they were going forward and might even be turning into paying propositions.

With the prospect of Romagna's five thousand dancing before my eyes, I took a taxi from Montparnasse Station to the Forum des Halles.

It was one of those days that Paris produces every now and then: blue sky of a tremendous lucidity; formal white clouds scattered here and there in perfect taste by the Master Designer; the Seine a glittering silver snake flowing beneath the Pont Mirabeau, Pont de Grenelle, Pont de Bir-Hakeim, Pont d'Iéna, the elegant bridges that segment its length.

It was a resplendent day. The crowds were out in force. In the Forum and on the broad terrace in front of the Beaubourg, two musical groups were vying for attention. One group was dressed in the national costume of Brittany and was doing folk dances. The other group was South American, and was composed of two lead guitars, a bass guitar, and a soprano guitar.

I'm a fool for a good huapanga, so I went over to catch their number. I recognized Juanito, the Paraguayan bandleader from El

Mango Encantado. He had on one of those frilled white shirts with puffy sleeves.

Slipping his maracas into his belt, he flashed me a big smile. "Meet me after this set, 'Ob. I have news for you about Alex."

"You got it," I said. "I'll be having a drink at the Père Tranquile."

It's amazing how easy it is to pick up information if you know where to hang out. I think I can say without exaggeration that I am one of the most skilled hangers-out in the western hemisphere. It's a talent like any other, of course, and it's main ingredient is patience.

"So hi there, keed," Juanito said, twenty minutes later, leaving his buddies to pass the hat. "How you been keepin', huh?"

In addition to the ruffled shirt, Juanito was wearing black skintight bullfighter pants, Nike running shoes, and he had a blue and white polkadot bandanna knotted casually around his neck like Jon Voigt in *Midnight Cowboy.* This time he gave me his boyish grin rather than his Apache scowl.

"Listen, 'Ob, you still wanna get in touch with Alex?"

Juanito's big grin and shiny eyes told me that this was going to cost me. Maybe dearly. Ain't nobody love you like the guy who's going to take you off.

I temporized. "Well," I said, "I'm not exactly *looking* for him. I mean, I'd like to *see* him as long as I'm in Paris anyway, but if I don't, well, it's no big deal, you know what I mean?"

Juanito's face fell. I could see the adding machine in his brain taking thirty percent off the price he was going to ask me for his most probably bogus information.

"Come on, 'Ob," he said, putting up the grin again, "I know you gotta find Alex and it's worth something, isn't it?"

I allowed as how there might be a few francs in it, nothing to get excited about, but something.

"What's it worth to you if I can take you right to him?"

"Can you?" I asked.

"Not just yet, 'Ob, but soon. But first you gotta tell me, what's it worth to you."

I favored him with a hard look. "Juanito, if you can lead me right to Alex without a whole lot of crapping around, I'll give you two hundred dollars American and I'll do you a favor."

"What favor?"

"I won't tell the gendarmes you haven't got a green card."

He looked just ever so slightly poleaxed. "How you know about that?"

"I don't reveal my sources." Nor my lucky guesses.

"Make it five hundred, OK? I got people to take care of."

I was going to tough it out, but then I figured, what the hell, it's someone else's money, because bribes paid in the line of duty are chargeable to the client, or possibly to both clients, if it turns out that way.

"All right," I said. "When do we do this?"

"Meet me tonight in front of Sainte-Eustache. You know where that is?"

"Of course I know. What do you take me for, a tourist?" I could always look it up.

"OK, see you then."

"Wait a minute; what time?"

"Let's make it midnight, OK, 'Ob?"

"Fine," I said. "But just do me one favor, OK?"

"Sure, 'Ob," he said, smiling and looking a little puzzled.

"Stop calling me 'Ob. You're South American; you have no excuse for not aspirating. Try it, H-O-B."

" '-O-B," Juanito said.

"Much better," I told him. *"Hasta mas tarde."* I walked away thinking, midnight, hmm; wonder if that means anything.

VICO IN PARIS 33

Later in the afternoon I was sitting on a bench near the Seine when who should show up but Vico. He sat down on the other end of the bench and didn't say anything.

This was Sunday. I remembered that yesterday had been Vico's race in the sailing contest in Honfleur. This was the day Vico was supposed to pay me Frankie Falcone's money for the boards, assuming Vico had won. By looking at him I couldn't tell how it had gone. He didn't have the bright-eyed look of a winner. Nor did he have the down-at-the-ears look of a loser. Under the circumstances, I decided to ask.

"So how did the sailboard contest go?" I asked him.

"I am not interested in your jokes," Vico said.

"What are you talking about?"

"You know very well."

"No, I do not know," I told him. "What am I supposed to know?"

Vico glowered. "You know that I did not compete in the Honfleur race."

"How would I know that?"

"Because you stole the boards," Vico said. His face contorted. He sobbed, "Oh, you bastard! My big chance, and you can't even trust me for a few lousy hours!"

"Somebody stole your boards? How? When?"

"They were supposed to have been brought to the hotel from the airport. They never arrived."

"But who took them? Surely someone must have seen."

"A large man in a chauffeur's uniform. That's what the porter told me."

"Not me, obviously. I don't even own a chauffeur's outfit."

"You could have employed such a person to steal my boards," Vico pointed out.

I didn't bother pointing out the irony in him accusing me of stealing boards that he himself had stolen from my employer. A guy like that was beyond irony. Instead I asked, "Why would I steal them?"

"So that you can return the boards to your client Falcone."

"Good idea," I told him. "I should have thought of that yesterday. But I had already agreed to wait. Don't you remember?"

Vico shrugged.

"Vico, wake up," I told him. "I did not steal your boards. Got it?"

"It doesn't matter whether I got it or not," Vico said. "The problem is not what I think, the problem is what will my partners think."

"This is the first time I've heard about your partners. I thought it was you against the world in this sailboarding venture."

"Well, I exaggerated slightly," Vico said. "The point is, I *do* have partners and they do not like this development. Missing the Honfleur sailing trials is bad enough. But what about the other European sailboarding events? Amsterdam next week, and then Garmisch, Lake Constance, Maggiore? It is important that I sail in these events."

"I sympathize," I said. "But you should have paid for the boards in the first place, instead of smuggling them into France on a fishing boat."

"You know about that? Mr. Draconian, I made a bad mistake doing that. But I was forced to it. Back in Ibiza, I entrusted my brother, Enrique, who is also the bookkeeper of Marisol, to send Señor Falcone his check. But Enrique went off with it instead to San Sebastián, where he has probably gambled it away by now."

"Whatever happened, you didn't pay. You stole the boards."

"I had a panic," Vico said. "And I was unable to contact my partners, who were traveling to Europe to watch me race."

"Partners? You hadn't mentioned them before."

"Well, I do have partners, and I have talked with them and we have decided to pay your client, Mr. Falcone, for the boards now, immediately."

"Really? I thought you couldn't spare a sou until you won a race."

"That is technically correct. But my partners have some money, luckily. We don't blame you, Mr. 'Ob, for taking back the boards. But I really need them now. Hence, *voilà*, the payment."

He removed a thick manilla envelope from an inner pocket and handed it to me. Within was a wad of bills. I riffled through them quickly. There were American and French bank notes, and some Sterling. Quite a bit of everything.

"How much is here?" I asked.

"Twenty-five thousand dollars. You can pay Mr. Falcone and keep the rest for yourself."

"Why would you do that for me, Vico?" I asked.

"Because I like you, Mr. 'Ob. And because I must have those boards back and you seem to be the key to obtaining them."

"I already told you, I don't know anything about who took your—or rather Frankie's—sailboards."

"All that is understood," Vico said, with that deadpan softness that Spaniards sometimes get just before they blow the bugle and storm the barricades. "I level no accusations. Just have someone deliver the boards to the following address"—he took out a slip of paper and gave it to me—"in the next forty-eight hours, and everyone will be satisfied."

"I'll do what I can," I said, pocketing the money. "But I can't promise anything."

"Please see that the boards arrive at that address," Vico said. "For your own sake."

He rose to go.

I rose, too. "Are you threatening me?"

"Not me. I am a nonviolent person. It is my partners that we both must worry about." He left.

The slip of paper gave an address outside of Paris. I put it into my wallet. Then I telephoned Nigel Wheaton and arranged to meet him at Harry's New York Bar.

"I understand the problem," Wheaton said, after I told him about my conversation with Vico.

"Do you think someone could have stolen the sailboards who had anything to do with the rest of this? Or was it random?"

"Difficult situation, old boy. But I'll see what I can do."

Wheaton smiled and alarm bells went off in my mind. I tend to believe that my friends remain exactly as they were when I saw them last. But I was always wrong. I wasn't how or who I had been ten years ago; why should they be?

"Nigel," I said, "you don't happen to own a chauffeur's uniform, do you?"

"Certainly not, old boy," Nigel said. "See you soon." He walked to the door, then turned. "But I know where I could get one in a hurry, of course." And with that he was on his way.

I knew nothing about what Nigel was doing these days. I had just breezed into Paris and assumed that time had stayed nicely frozen, and everything and everyone had stayed the same. But it hadn't. It couldn't have. So what did Nigel do when he wasn't working for me? And who could I find this out from?

When I returned to Le Cygne, the concierge told me there had been a phone call for me. A certain Jean-Claude had asked me to contact him as soon as possible. I went to my room and telephoned.

The phone was answered by what sounded like a large, redheaded woman speaking French with a strong Spanish accent. The Spanish are the *schvartzers* of France. They supply the concierges to the second- and third-rate Parisian hotels. On the social scale they are one step above the Algerians, who sweep the streets at night with brooms made of bundles of twigs. I switched to Spanish, and heard the usual Spanish complaint about the coldness of the French people and the blandness of their food. After she learned that I didn't know anyone in Albacete, she told me that Jean-Claude had gone out, but was very eager to speak to me. I gave her the number of my hotel.

I still had an hour and a half before meeting Juanito. So I bathed and took a nap. You may think that I do a lot of napping. It isn't so, actually. Other detectives nap a lot, too. They just don't tell you about it. But I have determined to write a true account of my case. So let it stand.

I set my Casio wrist alarm for 11:45 P.M., lay down and fell asleep almost at once. All too soon the alarm went off, and my struggle to program the watch into stopping its damnable chiming woke me up nicely. I put on a dark blue cotton sports shirt and my lightweight khaki sports jacket with the many pockets, and went out into the warm and murmurous Paris night.

SAINTE-EUSTACHE 34

A BRIEF CONFERENCE with the concierge at my hotel told me all I needed to know concerning the location of Sainte-Eustache. It was practically around the corner. I left Le Cygne and walked down Rue Rambuteau, past the Forum des Halles, to Sainte-Eustache near the Bourse. It was a great Gothic cathedral, built to rival Notre-Dame. Rising above the pork and fish stalls of the quartier, its flying buttresses and rose windows were visible in the light-filled Paris night. It was just going on midnight when I arrived: I could hear the *horloge,* the great clock four meters high and weighing over a ton, sounding the hour from the nearby *passage de l'horloge.*

Within seconds of my arrival Juanito showed up. Or perhaps he had been there all along, waiting for me. He wore his Spanish musician's costume of earlier, to which he had added a smart waist-length dark blue cape, giving him slightly the resemblance to a St-Cyr student.

"Ah, amigo, come with me," Juanito said, leading me into Sainte-Eustache.

The nave was high, and the vaulting, with its hanging keystones, was little short of flamboyant. We walked toward the altar, past the Lady Chapel and Colbert's tomb. The place was a quick survey in French history. Richelieu, Molière and Madame de Pompadour had been baptized here. Louis XIV had his first communion here, and this was where they had held the funerals of La Fontaine, Mirabeau, and the previously mentioned Molière.

"Where are we going?" I whispered.

"When did you last make confession?" Juanito whispered back.

"Hey," I told him, "I'm a Jew; we don't do that sort of thing."

"Then this will be a new experience for you." He led me around to a confessional booth. I eyed it with distaste.

"What is this?" I asked. These South Americans sometimes have a strange sense of humor.

"Go in," Juanito said, indicating the booth. "You will see."

I didn't like it, but what the hell, I went into the booth. The curtain closed off the view of the outside. Leaning forward, I found the little trap door that you open in order to converse with the priest. I slid it open. From the other side I could hear a rustling sound, as of a priest adjusting his gown or whatever it is he wears.

After a while a soft voice said, *"Oui, mon fils?"*

I shrugged my shoulders in impatience. This situation was definitely putting me off. The great shadowy church, the fantastical shapes, the massed candles, the stately sculptures, the odor of incense and piety, all were combining to give me a quick case of nervous indigestion. This was definitely not my Paris. I managed to restore a measure of sanity to the scene by saying, in conversational tones, "Hi, I'm Hob Draconian; to whom am I having the pleasure of confessing?"

"They told me you were a bit of a fool," a nonclerical voice growled from the other side of the partition.

"I'm not fool enough to set up meetings in confession booths," I said. "What is this, some kind of weird kick with you? And who are you, anyhow?"

"I must not be seen talking to you," the voice said. "This place seems as secure as any I could think up on short notice, and it has the advantage of being close to your hotel."

"Yes, that is handy," I said. "Of course, you could have come to my hotel room and I would have sent up for a few bottles of wine, and we could have conducted this thing in a civilized manner. And I suppose it is secure, as long as the priest doesn't start wondering why we're playing in his booth."

"The priest is in Marrakesh, on holiday," the voice said. "Don't you think we know how to arrange these matters?"

"I don't know. Who are you?"

"It is not necessary for you to know that."

"You're right," I said, "and it also isn't necessary for me to be doing this." I stood up. "If you want to continue this conversation you'll find me at Au Pied du Cochon next door. I'll probably be ordering a *gratinée.*"

"Not so fast," the presumably ersatz priest hissed. "How much will you pay for information about Alex?"

I sat down again. At last we were moving into reality.

"I'd have to hear the information first before I can judge its worth to me."

"My informant will require a minimum payment of five hundred American dollars if you judge the information to be of value. Is that agreeable?"

"Yes," I said, "but only if."

"Can you give me a hundred dollars now to show your good intentions?"

"Don't be ridiculous," I said.

"All right. Follow me."

ESTEBAN 35

We left Sainte-Eustache, the bogus priest and I, and walked down Rue de la Truanderie and then into Rue St-Denis. Snack bars, boutiques, sex shops, cafés, all were out in full force. I took a look at my companion. He was tall, with a yellowish-green complexion, raptor eyes and a Pancho Villa moustache. What I had taken for a cassock turned out to be a poncho.

"Have you got a name?" I asked him, "or do I just refer to you as the bogus priest?"

"Call me Ishmael," he said. "No, don't call me Ishmael, that's just a nervous reflex from the literature course I took last year at the New School in New York."

"Was it a good course?" I asked. I mean, you have to say something.

"I particularly liked the buxom young Jewish girls who attended," he said. "For the rest of it, I'll be happy when I can stop thinking about white whales. You may call me Esteban."

We walked on a ways in companionable silence. At last I asked him, "Where, exactly, are you taking me?"

By this time we had come to the shadowy stretches around the Fountain of Innocents. It is a place of bad memory, where, during the siege of Paris by Henri of Navarre in 1590, it is said that the dead rose out of the great charnel house which encircled this area and danced in the streets. Now it is a tourist attraction by day, and at night a place for clandestine arrangements and small deals in contraband.

"I suppose this will do as well as any other place," Esteban said.

Two figures detached themselves from the strollers circling the fountain. I didn't like the way they came directly toward me, separating so as to approach me one from each side. Nor did I like the way Esteban stepped away from me, his hand going into a pocket of his cape and coming out with something that glittered and was not a harmonica.

"Esteban," I said, "I misjudged you."

"Indeed?"

"I took you for an honest grifter and you turn out to be a *momzer* of deepest hue."

Esteban chuckled. "*Momzer!* I had forgotten the exotic dialect of New York. How I wish I could speak it idiomatically."

"If we made a deal," I said, "I could tutor you in Yiddish."

"I have taken an instant liking to you, Hob," Esteban said, effortlessly aspirating my name. "I regret having to put you through this more than you can imagine. Politics is a cruel mistress."

"Stop trying to sound villainous," I responded. "Listen, Esteban, seriously, let's you and me sit down somewhere and talk it out. No situation is unworkable."

"If only it were up to me," Esteban said, with that melancholy expression South Americans sometimes get when they are forced to hurt someone they really like. "But my hands are tied; this is an action order direct from El Grupo Blanco."

"Oh, it came direct from El Grupo Blanco," I said.

"Yes, that is correct."

"Hell," I said, "why didn't you tell me that in the first place? In that case it's all right for you to do whatever the hell you want with me, as long as Grupo Blanco authorized it. Now honestly, admit it, Esteban, isn't that a silly position?"

I suppose my words were over their heads. Without even

acknowledging what I'd said, Esteban's two henchmen or whatever-you-call-them converged on me from two sides.

I made my play. I bolted through the widest gap between my three surrounders, in the direction of the Boulevard Sébastopol. Fear lent speed to my flashing limbs.

Unfortunately, I didn't make it.

They had been ready for me. As I rushed by, one of them stuck out a leg, the other one swung his arm. Just like they'd rehearsed this before. Quasars exploded in my brain. My legs turned to soap bubbles. I heard a high, shrill singing in my head. I never felt when I hit the pavement.

BOIS DE BOULOGNE 36

IT IS CURIOUS how the Spanish world continues to impinge on my life though I have left Ibiza far behind. There must be something about the mentality that appeals to me, makes me seek out the arid zeitgeist of Hispanicism. Countries exist as models for our minds, and they give us coloration beyond our individual mannerisms. My tie with Spain was profound, ironic, and as delusional as the adventures of the great Quixote himself, my progenitor.

These were my thoughts as I lay slumped against one side of the interior of what seemed to be a large touring car. I decided to feign unconsciousness for a while. Through the fringe of my narrowed eyelids I could make out two large men in the back with me, facing me on jump seats. Beyond them, I saw Esteban sitting beside the driver. The driver wore a driver's cap. You gotta hand it to the South Americans; they've got style. Of course, what they were doing kidnapping me was something that defied even my powers of fantastical association. And what in hell was El Grupo Blanco, anyhow, and what did they want from me?

The two men in the jump seats were talking together in low tones. They were speaking a language I'd never heard. Occasionally, one of them made a remark to Esteban, and he responded in the same language.

It occurred to me that maybe they weren't Latins at all. Sounded a little like Albanian to me. Or maybe one of those Macedonian dialects that have been around since the days of Alexander the Great.

Already we had gone from the center of Paris to the Périphérique, the ring road that surrounds the city. We turned into the Porte de la Villette and went west. The traffic thinned out here. We swept around the northern limit of the city and turned south past Porte Maillot, then continued another mile or so and exited at the Porte Dauphine. We were in the Bois de Boulogne now, the large, carefully cultivated forest on Paris' western side.

As we drove through its shady promenades, I could see an occasional prostitute parading the sidewalk, wearing furs with little under them. We reached the Allée de Longchamp, where the male prostitutes hang out. At last, we passed the grounds of the Racing Club of France and came to a stop just past the heights of Pré Catelan, in marshy ground close to the Lac Inférieur. This is where the Paris gangs are said to dispose of the bodies of their victims.

"All right, Hob," Esteban's firm, well-aspirated voice said. "This is it—end of the line, as you Americans say."

No sense feigning unconsciousness any longer. It looked like the real thing might be mine soon enough: that Big Sleep that Jim Morrison sang about.

"Please get out of the car," Esteban said.

I obeyed quietly, with no clever wisecrack for once. It disturbed me that Esteban hadn't warned me not to try to escape. It was like he didn't care what I tried, because he already had his plans for me.

Esteban and his helpers formed up around me and led me deeper into the bosky woods. It was a clear night. Through the branches I could make out Orion overhead. Our feet made delicate crunching sounds, as we crossed the sward or whatever it was. One of the men had a nasty head cold. He kept on blowing his nose into a white handkerchief. I couldn't think of any way to use that to my advantage, but at least I hadn't given up yet.

At length we came to a little clearing. We stopped here. Esteban said, "OK, let's talk."

He made a gesture with his hand. His two helpers backed up a ways. That felt marginally better. Not really good enough to restore our relationship, but definitely a start.

"My frien'," Esteban said, "maybe it's not such a good idea you looking for Alex."

"Funny you should say that," I said. "I was just beginning to think that myself."

"Really?" said Esteban.

"Yeah, I've given it a lot of thought," I told him. "This Alex thing is *un poquito complicado, verdad?* Not really my sort of thing at all. I was just about deciding to write it off and go home to my ex-wives."

"That's a very good idea," Esteban said.

"He's not so dumb as he looks," one of the henchmen remarked.

I let that pass. "Problem is, if I give up the job, I don't have any money to get home with."

Esteban stared at me. Then he gave a short, grunting laugh. "Señor Draconian, you amaze me. Are you trying to get me to pay you money to give up this case? One would think you would be grateful just to walk away with your life."

"I'm grateful for that, of course," I said. "Don't get me wrong. But frankly, I didn't figure you were actually going to kill me."

"How did you come to that conclusion?"

"For one thing, El Grupo Blanco wouldn't approve. Not really. You know how often they change their minds. Right now, discretion is the order of the day. Don't make waves; otherwise you'll compromise a lot of carefully laid plans."

"What do you know about El Grupo?" Esteban asked.

"What I know is my business. I'm not going to reveal what I know to you or anyone else. That's protection for you, too, you know."

"You take a lot of chances," Esteban muttered. "I don't know; perhaps we're safer with you dead."

"Don't you believe it," I said. "For one thing, if you kill me, you compromise Juanito. Inspector Fauchon of the Paris Police knows my every movement. He has me under constant surveillance. Don't think that this little kidnapping has gone unnoticed. Fauchon and his men are ready to move against you at any time."

"No one could have followed us," Esteban said. But he didn't sound sure. How can you be sure?

"They don't have to tail you direct." I told him. "If I know Fauchon, he planted a bug on your car as soon as he saw how things were going. He's subtle, Fauchon is. But I guess that's the sort of thing you'd expect of the French."

Esteban turned to his helpers and they talked in the language I didn't understand. Listening more carefully, I decided it wasn't Albanian. Sounded more like one of the Turkish languages to me, Azerbijaini, maybe. It wasn't until later that I learned it was Guaraní, the main Indian language of Paraguay.

"Are you going to stop looking for Alex?" Esteban demanded.

"I'll think about it. Meanwhile cross my palm with silver, or paper notes, and I'll try to make it easy on you when this whole ball of wax comes unstuck."

"This is ridiculous," Esteban said. "You are in no position to demand anything."

"That's not the way I see it," I told him. "Come on, Esteban, pay up. It's not your money, anyhow. It belongs to El Grupo Blanco. They won't even notice a few thousand dollars if you mark it down as petty cash."

"A few thousand? That is impossible. We are operating on a very tight budget. It is very expensive for us South Americans to live in Paris."

"Well, it's up to you," I said. "Hell, I never asked you to bribe me. Do what you please. But please do get on with it. Fauchon is probably sick of crouching in the bushes, and I've got more important things to do than hang around the Bois de Boulogne all night with you."

Esteban held another hurried conference. Then he took out his wallet.

"I'll give you ten thousand francs," he said. "But you must promise to stop looking for Alex."

I took the bills and stuck them in my pocket. "Actually, Esteban, you're better off with *me* looking for him instead of someone else. I have to find Alex because that's my job. But I'm also a friend of Alex, and I'll do the best I can for him."

"You said you would stop looking!" Esteban said. He sounded genuinely outraged. These hijacking types have a pathetic belief that they can lie all they want; everyone else is obliged to keep his word.

"I have to go on looking, but I won't try very hard."

Esteban must have realized he'd met his match in the art of obfuscation. His retort was weak, "Just remember, you have been warned. Watch yourself. The next time we have to talk with you, it could be for keeps." It was pitiable, his blustering that way, but I guess he was trying to save face.

As Esteban and his friends started to walk back to their car, I called out, "Hey, how about a ride back into Paris?"

"Get a ride back with your friend Fauchon!" he cried.

Soon I heard their car start up and drive away.

I heard a rustle of underbrush. Out of the bushes stepped Inspector Fauchon with a plainclothes detective beside him.

"Very good, 'Ob," Fauchon said. "We're keeping an eye on those fellows. But how did you know that I was close by?"

"I didn't know, really," I said. "But it was what I wished for more than anything else in the world."

"It is nice when dreams come true," Fauchon agreed. "You may turn over the ten thousand francs to me."

"Hey, come on! I went through quite a bit of unpleasantness to get it!"

"You'll get it back, at the end of the case," Fauchon said. "Marcel, give him a receipt."

The other cop, a tall cadaverous plainclothesman with a crew cut, got out a pocket notebook, scrawled something, handed it to me. I gave him the money. Easy come; easy go.

JEAN-CLAUDE AND NIGEL; ABOUT ALEX 37

JEAN-CLAUDE WAS WAITING outside my hotel when I drove up in Fauchon's Peugeot. He stepped back discreetly into the shadows until Fauchon and I had made our farewell salutations.

"Well, Inspector," I said, "thank you very much for rescuing me. Actually, I had the situation well in hand. But a little backup is always nice."

Fauchon gave a shrug and made a grimace. "Take care of yourself, 'Ob. I think you are—how do you Americans say it—playing in a sticky wicket over your head."

"That's what we say, all right," I said. "I suppose you want me to report to you at regular intervals on everything I've seen, heard or done concerning Alex?"

"Oh, no," Fauchon said, chuckling. "Just carry on as you are doing. You're not a hard man to follow. And it's a change for us from the usual routine."

"Would you mind telling me," I asked, "what it is about Alex that has excited the attention of the Paris Police? Is he wanted for something?"

"Not as far as I know," Fauchon said. "But of course, who knows what the morrow will bring, non?"

He strolled back to his car whistling "Auprès de ma Blonde" in his own inimitable fashion.

After Fauchon had driven off, Jean-Claude came out of the

shadows, mouth downturned, eyebrow raised. I knew I was in for some tedious French irony, so I forestalled it by shrugging and saying, "Come up to the room. We'll have a glass of wine and exchange gossip, n'est-çe pas?"

Jean-Claude shrugged and followed me into the hotel.

Nigel Wheaton was already in my room and had helped himself to a healthy tote of the Haig & Haig I'd bought on the airplane. Nigel likes to just show up like that. He claims that subterfuge and lock-picking keep him in practice for more serious things. This evening he was wearing his Harris tweed jacket, cotton twill officer's trousers and highly polished Spanish boots.

"Ah there, dear boy! None the worse for your little outing to Honfleur, I see."

"That's something we have to talk about."

"Now, 'Ob," Jean-Claude said, "I tried to warn you. I telephoned you, left word it was urgent."

"And then you weren't in when I called back."

"I had gone down to the café for a pack of Gauloises. Why didn't you phone back?"

I was unable to find a crushing rejoinder for that, so I contented myself with pouring a shot of scotch, swirling it moodily in my toothbrush glass for a moment or two, then tossing it down. "That's better," I said, and then, annoyingly enough, I had a coughing fit and Jean-Claude had to pat me on the back.

"Get your greasy paws off me," I growled. "I always cough when I drink. Jean-Claude, just what in hell was it you were going to tell me when you telephoned?"

"I was going to warn you not to get into a car with any South Americans."

"And how did you know to tell me that?"

"I found out something late this afternoon. Didn't I, Nigel?"

"Yes, I'd say that you most certainly did," Wheaton said. "Do you have anything to munch on while I consume your excellent scotch? Cheese sticks would be nice."

I don't know what it is about Paris. Nobody seems to get anything done without food entering into it.

"Gee," I said, "I'm clean out of cheese sticks. Jean-Claude, why don't you telephone Le Zinc down the street and ask them to send up some sandwiches."

Jean-Claude looked at me as if I had gone crazy. "French cafés do not deliver!"

"They do for Maigret!" I countered.

"Oh, never mind," Nigel said. "But you used to keep a better table in Ibiza."

"That was when Katie was cooking for me."

"What a hand that girl had with Chinese spareribs!" Wheaton said.

I didn't want to get into it. I turned to Jean-Claude. "What did you learn?"

"I have a friend," Jean-Claude said, "who is a waiter at El Mango Encantado. He overheard a group of these gauchos talking. He said they were discussing Alex."

"What were they saying?"

"He couldn't make it out. It was in a language my friend didn't know."

"Could he ascertain their attitude toward Alex?"

"Yes, of course. We discussed that. He said that they were noncommittal."

"That makes about as much sense as anything else in this case."

I reached for one of Nigel's cigarettes, then remembered that I had given up smoking a few months ago, or possibly a few weeks ago. Then I took it anyway, since it didn't look right now as if I'd live long enough to develop lung cancer.

"I have a little more information for you," Nigel said. "Do you know what Alex was doing in the last several years?"

"Selling underwater real estate in Florida, I'd imagine."

"You'd be very wrong. Alex was employed by Aaron, Murphy, Steinmetz and Frunken."

"Lawyers?"

"Yes, but not a law firm. They are fund-raisers, Hob."

"Fund-raisers? You mean like for political campaigns and stuff?"

"Yes, that sort of thing. But for the last year or two they were working on a special project. A project that relates to the recent revelations about Iran and the Contras funding."

"Must I pry this out of you word by word?" I asked. "Forget about dramatic presentation, Nigel; just tell me the facts."

Nigel told me that Alex had left Europe about five years ago. With the help of his socially prominent Virginia family, he was able to get taken on by the Selwyn Group, a firm of professional fund-raisers. Several groups were involved in the private effort to raise money for the Contras. Alex had been very much of a junior lawyer in this effort. As matters had proceeded, he had started to worry. What was going on seemed to him to exist on the shady side of legality.

Then Attorney-General Meese belatedly blew the whistle. Investigative committees were formed; witnesses were called. Alex took stock of his situation. He hadn't liked it from the beginning. Too many people coming in and out of the office with conspiratorial looks on their faces. His superior, Tom Ogden, had told him straight along that he was all right, everything was covered, no one was going to have any trouble. But then the congressional investigations began. Casey, North, and Poindexter were asked to give testimony. Casey had a stroke and never recovered. McFarlane tried to commit suicide. Alex realized belatedly that it was time to look after his own ass.

Of course, he had been following Ogden's orders. There was nothing they could get him for. Not as long as Selwyn was there to testify.

Then Selwyn went into the hospital for triple bypass surgery. He came out of it in good shape and was recovering nicely until three weeks later when suddenly he died.

After Selwyn's death, everything changed rapidly. Selwyn had had a lot of friends in high places. But that didn't do Alex any good now. The investigating committees were looking for people to fit into the conspiratorial structure they had uncovered. Alex began to feel the heat.

Ogden's papers would clear Alex, of course. But suddenly these papers were no longer forthcoming. Alex learned via the grapevine that Selwyn's widow might have done something with them. She was taking all necessary steps to protect her husband's good name, and his sizable pension that came to her now that he was dead.

The Selwyn Group disbanded. Alex took his separation check and thought long and hard about what to do next. It looked like, if and when the committee got around to calling him, he could find himself facing criminal charges. As a lawyer, he figured he might get from two to five years for conspiracy and other counts.

He discussed the matter with his secretary. She had been with him from the beginning of his working for Selwyn. His secretary advised him to get out of town. It was by no means certain that the committee would call him up. But they would be likelier to if he stayed in Washington. Better he should get away now, while no one was looking for him, and take an extended holiday somewhere abroad. Like Paris, for example.

Alex decided to go immediately. He emptied out his bank account. It wasn't much—the government had put a hold on his main account. He still maintained a checking account in Paris, at Crédit Suisse. There was only a few hundred dollars in it. It would have to do. He signed an authorization for his secretary to withdraw his money when it was released. And took off.

Nigel paused to pour himself another drink. I said, "Where did you learn all this?"

"Rachel told me. As you might have surmised, she was Alex's secretary."

"She never told me all that," I said.

Nigel looked extremely pleased with himself. "That's because you lack the intimate touch, old boy. Kate used to remark on it to me, back in the old days."

I let that pass. "When did Rachel tell you this stuff?"

"Last night, dear boy, when I went round to her hotel to interview her. She's a rather sweet little thing."

"Damn it," I said, "she should have told me all this at the start. What sort of a mug does she take me for? I think Rachel and I had better have this out at once."

I reached for the telephone. Nigel said lazily, "If you're calling her hotel, I'm afraid you won't find her in."

"Where is she?"

"I thought she'd be more comfortable in my place. Did you ever see my digs near the Panthéon? Just off St-Michel, a dear little place. She told me she hasn't had a decent meal since coming to Paris. Really, Hob, you've been neglectful."

I stared at Nigel, outraged for the moment. Then I had to laugh. I had forgotten Nigel's womanizing tendencies. Maybe it was the plummy British upper-class accent, or the military bearing, or the air of amused worldliness. Whatever, the women always seemed to go for him.

"All right, Nigel," I said. "You've done well. But you haven't found out what I really need to know. Namely, where is Alex now?"

Jean-Claude smoothed his moustache with a supercilious finger and said, "As for zat, I expect to have an answer for you within twenty-four hours."

"Tell me about it," I told him.

"But I just have. You don't think I'm going to tell you the names of my informants, eh?"

"No, of course not; silly of me. Jean-Claude, is this for real or are you shucking me again?"

"Qu'est-çe que ç'est, *'shucking'?"*

"It means, in this instance, to tell an untruth in hope that it will come true."

"I would not do that," Jean-Claude said. "Trust me, 'Ob. Tomorrow evening I will be able to take you to Alex."

"Great," I said.

"I will require, of course, an advance to take care of my informants."

"I could use a little front money too, Hob," Nigel said. "I more or less promised I'd buy Rachel the best cassoulet in Paris."

"Then let her pay for it herself."

"Now, Hob, don't be that way. Let me pay. You can add it to her account."

With an ill grace I paid them both. We parted with mutual expressions of esteem, somewhat muted on my part.

After they were gone, I tried Yvette again. We arranged to meet for lunch tomorrow. She might be able to tell me something. In any event, I was glad that Nigel hadn't seen her first.

GOURMET PRISON 38

IF YOU THINK French hotels are bad, you should try their prisons. At least they gave me a cell alone. I had been more than a little anxious when the guard led me down the flagstoned corridor, with prisoners leering and catcalling from their cells on either side. French prisons are really old. They were building and rebuilding these things back when North America was still an Indian reservation. And there's something about old European prisons. Hundreds of years of terror and misery permeate the soiled cobblestones of my cell. They give off an aura, these places that have been so long dedicated to retaining people against their wills. An old prison site is probably worse than any other contamination, because it's spiritual, a poisonous effluvium of mood that saps the will of even the bravest prisoner.

And I was not exactly the bravest. I think I've already explained that macho is not my thing. Nor am I accustomed to being hoisted out of my bed just before dawn by three grim-faced Paris Special Forces policemen, who looked ready to fight the Battle of Algiers all over again on my body.

They gave me time to make a hasty *toilette,* but not enough time to fasten my shoelaces. Nor to zip up my fly. One of them on either arm, the third opening doors, we marched through the hotel. The prosperous burghers in the lobby, with their simpering Mädchen standing by in their overstuffed dirndls, gave me reproving looks as I was half marched, half carried, out into the early Paris morning. No doubt in the minds of the onlookers, I was guilty of whatever the police were taking me away for; because after all, do the gendarmes pluck innocent people out of their beds? Remembering that livid frieze of accusatory faces, I had the passionate desire to grind them all into the dirt. For a moment I longed for the revolution of a proletariat with teeth such as the world has never yet seen.

They piled me into the ominous high-backed blue Citröen van that is always to be seen at student demonstrations, two of them in back with me, daring me with their eyes to complain, to protest, to make any move or gesture that would justify their "beating a little sense into me." I sat mute, my head hanging low, taking on the posture of one who, to an expert physiognomist, as all the French consider themselves, would appear to exhibit indisputable postural proof of guilt.

We pulled up at the outer gate to La Santé, the big prison in the center of Paris. The police sentries saluted and pulled back the iron gates with their curved and gilded tops. We came to a stop in an interior courtyard. I was swept into a cramped and sweaty room filled with policemen. A sergeant at a desk had a brief argument with one of my captors, in Corsican, I believe, since the only word I could make out was "Ecco!" said by the sergeant as he threw his hands in the air while my captors steered, pushed and dragged me deeper inside.

And that is why I linger here, alone and palely loitering, though the sedge is withered from the soth and no lawyers ring. Excuse me, that was hysteria. But I really did want to see a lawyer. I wanted a French lawyer who would invoke whatever French jurisprudence uses in place of habeas corpus, to get me out of here, get me out of here, get me out of here. . . .

Sorry, there goes my hysteria again; it comes over me whenever I relive those days, even here, from the supposedly safe spot in which I am writing these memoirs. My cell was about four feet on a side, solid rock walls, little barred window about twelve feet straight up, a slop bucket (I later learned that plumbing troubles were frequent in this quartier), a small bench that looked as if it had been assembled by chimpanzees back at the beginning of time, and nothing more except a few messages scratched onto the wall. The only one I could make out read, simply, COURAGE! and it was signed, FRANCESCO ISSÁSAGA. A Basque name, I believe. But what did that matter?

A single naked lightbulb, caged in wire, hung by a long frayed cord from the high ceiling. I looked at it but it gave me no ideas. What was really annoying was that I had nothing to read. Funny how that's one of the first things a man thinks of when he finds himself in jail. My theory is that the taste for reading is so developed in some of us that it amounts to a veritable appetite on a par with eating, sleeping, fornicating, and sitting around feeling sorry for oneself. Most of us never suffer real linguistic deprivation, because, even if we are not actively reading, we are aware of the plethora of reading matter on all sides of us—newspapers, magazines, books, billboards, menus, calling cards, notices on telephone poles, and the like. Thus we are bathed daily in a sea of words, and we take care to be well provisioned when we undertake air, rail, or bus trips, or when we have to spend a lot of time on queues in public agencies trying to get our visas stamped. Prison is a form of travel, too, a foretaste perhaps, of that Great Waiting Room in the Sky which some say is the long-term destination of most of us. Yes, these are gloomy thoughts, but *que voulez-vous?* I'm in prison; I don't have to be cheerful.

There was nothing for me to do but sit quietly and put my thoughts in order. I believe it was Pascal who pointed out that most of the mischief in the world is due to man's inability to sit quietly in a room for any length of time. Now was my chance to try to solve the world's problems, at least in microcosm.

I adjusted my shoes and clothing, took off my jacket, folded it, put it down on the bench, sat down on it. No sooner had I done that than the heavy old-fashioned lock on the outside of my door turned with a grating sound, and the door flew open. I stood up rather hastily, because a horrid thought had gone through my mind. There is a famous scene in French literature and movies which portrays the criminal in his cell, waiting to hear whether he will be executed or pardoned. He waits, his eyes fastened on the door. Suddenly it flies open. Policemen rush in, seize him, and, despite his screams and struggles, drag him off to the guillotine. Pardon denied!

Yes, they still use the guillotine over here. Not that I was in immediate danger of that. There is generally a rather long and complicated trial before it is brought into play. But I had forgotten that, or, rather, I had considered it but had thought that maybe *they* had forgotten about it.

And so I was prepared to act like my predecessors, all the convicted, guilty and innocent alike, who have been seized and carried through these portals to meet their ends in one of the more stylish executions still extant in the world today. But of course, what happened was nothing of the sort.

My visitor was a guard, dressed like all the others, but with one exception: instead of a round policeman's hat, he wore a tall, spotlessly white, rakishly curved to one side chef's hat.

"Good day, m'sieu," he said. "I am Henri, a representative of Le Repas Obigatoire of the Santé kitchens. I can take your dinner order now, m'sieu."

I was dumbfounded, but managed to retain sufficient sang froid to enquire, "What would you recommend?"

"Our fare is simple, but has won awards in *L'Incarcerátion,* the International Magazine of Prisons. *Potage parisien,* to start, accompanied by *le bloc de paté fois gras trufflée,* then *gigot de mouton de Sologne à l'eau,* accompanied by a medley of fresh asparagus and cut red peppers decorated with a sheen of finest olive oil. If m'sieu would prefer a fowl course, today we are featuring *pêche de caneton* in a delicate sauce of Montmorency cherries."

"I'll take it," I said. "The duck, I mean. If that's all right. Although, I'm not saying anything against the gigot. And I know you mentioned it first. So if you'd prefer—"

I was being cautious, not captious. I had no idea what this

chef-guard's behavior signified. France is a strange country, after all, especially when you are forced to deal with the French.

"The choice is entirely up to you," Henri said. "Might I recommend a little-known Grâves '82 which we managed to secure only last week?"

"By all means," I told him. "But tell me something—if I might ask a question?"

"But of course, m'sieu," Henri said.

"What is this all about?"

"M'sieu?" Henri said, evidently puzzled.

"Where I come from," I told him, "prisoners don't get to choose to order gourmet food from a guard in a chef's hat with a wine list in his pocket. I always knew that France was ultracivilized, but this is too much!"

"We do like to think of ourselves as civilized, m'sieu," Henri said, "but I can assure you this is not an everyday occurrence in the Paris prison system. It is just that this year we are celebrating the Year of the Prisoner. No, no, I didn't mean that last; just my little joke, m'sieu; the fact is, I am not at liberty to say whence comes this most excellent repast, this prison fare fit for an emperor. All will be revealed in due course, never fear."

Smiling, bowing, Henri departed from my cell, not forgetting to lock the door behind him. I sat back on my bench and permitted myself just the faintest degree of relaxation. It is hard to explain why I felt that sense of relief, but I will try to explain, since it is directly relevant to the strange events that lay immediately ahead of me.

It is my belief or let us say theory, that the actions of men are ruled to a very great extent by the Spirit of Place. What do I mean by Spirit of Place? I refer to the individuating specificity that certain geographic regions possess; in other words, the congeries of associations and interconnections that binds a place to its past, shapes its future, determines the behavior of its citizens, and even sets the tone of the adventures experienced by those who visit it.

Put even more simply: in Venice, Venetian things happen; in

Hoboken, Hobokenese things happen; and you can bet that in the stony mountainscapes of the Chiricahua, Apache things happen.

So it is with Paris, a city which draws you quickly into its zeitgeist. Paris has not a single aspect, of course. Multiform and multiplex, it presents a variety of faces, of possibilities, of moods. It all depends on which Paris you're traveling in. Or, more exactly, which Paris is traveling through you. Is it the Paris of Jean Valjean, of Victor Hugo, the Paris of Haussmann, the Paris of Danton, the Paris of the Comédie Française? The possibilities are many, but each of the choices is a French one, and all together represent the collective *moira* of the Gallic entity, the still-developing collection of tendencies that is France.

What I thought I had detected, as Henri the chef-cop bowed himself out, was the strong possibility that the ground rules for my situation were about to change. We were leaving the gritty world of detection and entering a new realm of farce, French farce, of which there's nothing sillier. Or so I hoped.

FAUCHON 39

"YVETTE!" I SAID. For I had been thinking about her, and now she was standing before me. She had that smile on her face. That certain smile. You know the smile I mean? The smile that tells you you're in play.

"Hi, babe," I said huskily. "I kinda thought it'd be you."

"Really?" Yvette said, also huskily.

"Vraiment," I replied. "Are you really the right one, the one and only, the one who was promised me long ago in another country?"

"Search no more," Yvette said. "Here I am, the eternal feminine dwelling in the ephemeral me."

"I love the way you talk," I said. "Where did you ever learn it?"

"At the Barbizon School of Metaphysical Shuck."

"Landsman!" I cried.

"Weimeraner!" she replied.

I reached out for her, touched her face. Encountered stubble. Opened my eyes. Beheld Inspector Fauchon, smiling patiently, lower lip outthrust, waiting with commendable patience until I had awakened completely and pulled myself together.

"Are you all right?" Fauchon asked me.

"Oh, sure, I'm great," I told him. "Has sentence been passed yet? Where are the authorities going to send me? Devil's Island?

New Caledonia? If I have a choice, I'd kinda like to do my time in the Château d'Îf. Great admirer of Dumas, you know."

"Control yourself," Fauchon said with paternal sternness. "Accompany me to my office. There has been a ridiculous mistake."

We went through corridors measureless to man, down to a sunless office on the second floor of the gloomy Gallic gaol in which I had been incarcerated. Fauchon told me to make myself comfortable in the big armchair he reserved for respectable visitors, and sent out for café au lait and croissants.

"Kind of you," I said, "but what about the gourmet dinner I ordered earlier from Henri, the chef-guard?"

Fauchon looked puzzled, then smiled with evident pleasure. "Ah, you make the ironic jest! Very good! You must have been hallucinating. Sorry, we have no gourmet service for the prisoners, but I would be happy to take you to a first-rate restaurant this evening in partial atonement for the silly error of my subordinates. You see, I told Jacques Lefevre, my subaltern, if that is the correct word, to go to your hotel and ask you to come in and see me. Jacques was unable to go himself; as he was leaving, word came in of some strange occurrences in the Rue Morgue, and so he detailed his batman, if that is the correct term, and his assistants. He told them to bring you in, and they, considering you a common criminal, made their usual rude entry into your hotel room. Again, *je suis desolé;* I do beg your forgiveness."

"No harm done," I murmured, accepting Fauchon's outstretched hand. The thought did occur to me that the entire thing might have been staged, the arrest and then the apology, in order that I might consider the benefits of cooperation.

"What did you want to see me about?" I asked.

"This is going to please you very much. We have located the whereabouts of your friend Alex Sinclair. Not so bad work on the part of Paris flatfeet, non?"

"No," I said. "Or rather, yes, very good indeed. When can I see him?"

Fauchon set fire to a Gauloise. Cigarette in the middle of his faded rosebud mouth, French blue eyes squinted against the smoke, he leaned toward to me and said, "Ah! As for that, I am afraid there is a difficulty."

ARNE; ALEX FOUND 40

Le Père Tranquile was crowded as usual, its outside café portion crowded with sunglassed light worshippers. I ordered an omelette and a bottle of Orangina, and sat gazing upon the crowd with a jaundiced and dyspeptic eye. At the moment I could say, with Hamlet, man delights me not, no, nor woman, neither.

Arne the mime came by, white face, painted rosebud clown's mouth, baggy black trousers and checkered W.C. Fields vest. He did his number for a while, then came over to my table and sat down.

"*Ça va?*" he enquired.

I made an Italian gesture denoting nothingness.

"As bad as that?" Arne said.

"Made none the better by my recent experience with your friend Esteban." I related to him briefly the events of the previous night in the Bois de Boulogne.

"I never said he was a friend of mine," Arne pointed out. "Anyhow, maybe he was kidding. These South Americans are great jokers."

"So I've noticed."

"Don't worry," Arne said. "Something will break soon."

"That's what I'm afraid of."

Arne went back to his miming, and left the world to darkness and to me. I sat there trying to figure out where the South Americans fit into the picture and trying to make sense out of what Fauchon had told me. This was the mood I was in when Nigel came strolling by, immaculate in summer whites, twirling a malacca cane, a panama hat tilted rakishly over one eye, his beard bristling heroically.

"What ho?" Nigel said, the very image of hateful bonhomie.

"Besmirch me your what ho's," I said.

"Ah, we're a bit peevish this afternoon, are we?" Nigel sat down, and, catching a waiter's eye with an ease that I found unpleasantly knowledgeable, ordered a gin and tonic.

"So, what's new?"

"Not much," I said. "Except that Alex has been located."

"Then the case is completed?"

"Not quite. I still have to see him and give him the money Rachel has for him."

"But that's a mere detail," Nigel said. "Why don't we go do it now?"

"Because there is, to quote Inspector Fauchon, a difficulty."

"Just a minute." Nigel took a long pull at his gin and tonic, found a dented cheroot in his engraved silver cigar case and lit up. Leaned back and crossed his legs. "OK, I'm ready for anything."

"Inspector Fauchon told me that he knows where Alex is. The difficulty is, he's promised Clovis not to tell anyone about it until Clovis has finished shooting his film."

Nigel groaned and took another gulp of his gin and tonic. "I'm not ready for this. Why did he promise such a thing to Clovis?"

"Clovis needs Alex in his film. Alex has appeared in two weeks' worth of shooting. It would be expensive to shoot all over again. But worse than that, Clovis wouldn't do it. You know his reputation. Either he shoots a film through from beginning to end or he abandons it."

"But what does that have to do with Alex? I mean, why can't people see Alex?"

"Fauchon told me that Clovis is worried because Alex has disappeared from the shooting schedule twice now, causing costly delays and turning the whole project on its ear. Now that he has Alex again, he's keeping him in seclusion until the final squences of the movie are filmed."

"In seclusion where?"

"That's the part that Fauchon promised Clovis he wouldn't tell. Not until the shooting's finished."

"But why would Fauchon do this for Clovis?"

"That takes a little explaining. You know that the French government, through its various grants and facilities, bankrolls most of the French films in production. Clovis' film has already cost the government close to ten million dollars. They'll recoup when it's released, of course, unless Clovis throws a fit and doesn't finish it. The Minister of Culture wants to see this film finished. As a matter of fact, his daughter is working on the production."

"Yvette?" Nigel asked.

"Of course, Yvette. So the thing is, important people want to see Clovis finish his movie. Alex is necessary to Clovis; Alex is not wanted for any crime, and so Fauchon figures if an American wants to drop out, there's no law against it."

"But he told you that Alex was all right?"

"Precisely. 'Nevaire bettaire' were his precise words. The French police have no reason to assume that any foul play is involved here. If a man wants to isolate himself and not answer his calls, well, they didn't arrest Howard Hughes, did they? That was Fauchon's example, not mine."

"So what do we do next?"

"What I considered doing," I said, "was having you and Jean-Claude kidnap Clovis and threaten him with hideous tortures until he revealed Alex's whereabouts."

"We'd need a car for that," Nigel said thoughtfully. "Also it would cost more."

"Forget it," I said. "That was hyperbole, and it's not actionable."

"Well, what *are* we going to do?"

"I," I said, "am going to telephone Clovis immediately and demand an explanation."

"Yes," Nigel said. "I think you should."

"See you later," I said, and went inside to use the telephone.

I went to the change desk and asked for a *jeton,* the small French coin that activates jeton-operated telephones. It was rather difficult catching the attention of the girl behind the cash register. She was having an involved discussion with one of the waiters, a sulky-faced little fellow with long poetic hair, about regional variations in *choucroute garni.* It was a talk too tedious to translate. I finally obtained the requisite coin and went below, to the lower level where the toilets are, the telephone booths, and the inevitable concierge.

This particular toilet attendant had basilisk eyes, harpy nose, iron-gray hair and bloodless lips. I sidled toward the telephone booth, intimidated instantly. "M'sieu?" she said, holding out a small hand towel. I realized at once that she thought I was going to the toilet. I could have explained to her that I merely wanted to use the telephone, but these people don't like explanations, only money, so I accepted the towel, tipped her ten francs, and went into the phone booth.

I could see her watching me through the tinted glass. I was beginning to feel just a little weirded out. A few hours in a cell at Santé doesn't really do all that much for your equilibrium. And mine is just a bit wonky even at the best of times.

"Yes, hello, who is calling?"

The suddenness of Clovis' voice in my ear startled me, even when it was coming to me through a telephone receiver in response to the number I had just dialed.

"Clovis? It is Hob."

"Who?"

" 'Ob!"

"Ah, why did you not say so at first? Where are you, why have you not contacted me; you missed a shoot yesterday, did you know that?"

I was still going to give him hell for holding out on me about Alex. But first I thought I'd better explain my own omissions.

"I was going to phone you this morning," I said. "Then these cops came and dragged me out of bed—"

"Wait," Clovis said.

"Pardon?"

"I want you to save that story. You can tell it on camera in the next filming."

"I'm sorry, Clovis, I don't seem to be tracking you."

"We are filming a key scene tonight," Clovis said. "During it, you will need to make a speech. It doesn't matter what you say because we will dub in our own lines later, after we know what the scene is all about. You are following this, non?"

"No. Sorry, I mean yes."

"Be there at 10:00 P.M. sharp. The entire cast will be present. This is the big one, kid. We're counting on you."

"Oh, don't worry," I said (fatuously, as I think now).

"Good. By the way, Alex sends regards. He looks forward to seeing you. At ten, then!"

He hung up. I sat in the booth holding the receiver and gaping at my reflection in the plate glass. For a moment I doubted myself, but then I pulled myself together. yes, he had said it. Alex! Tonight at ten!

There was a heavy tapping at the door of my telephone booth. It was the concierge. I opened the door and stepped out. "Madame?" I said.

"The towel," she said, whipping it out of my hands. "One does not take a towel into the telephone booth."

I considered trying to explain, but it was just too difficult. Easier to tip her another ten francs and head for the stairs.

Wait until Nigel hears this, I thought, a modest gloat arising in my chest.

Then I stopped in mid-step and slapped my forehead with the palm of my right hand. I had neglected to get the address of the shoot from Clovis.

9

TELEPHONES IN CAFÉS 41

Glimpses of Paris: rectangular white and blue street signs; Grill Self-Service; people carrying the long loaves of French bread known as baguettes; open-air neighborhood food markets under striped awnings and umbrellas; the haughty beauty of the produce, aware of itself as the prototype for still-life painting; long, low barges on the Seine—*les bateaux;* fishing on the Seine; Japanese tourists in neat business suits, much becameraed; and everywhere, love is in the air—the couples walking arm-in-arm, or arms entwined around each other's waist, pausing here and there to exchange a long kiss; orienting glimpses of the Eiffel Tower, Notre-Dame, the Montparnasse Tower, the Sacré-Coeur, Invalides, the Panthéon, the Luxembourg Gardens; the swirl of traffic around the Étoile, the Place de la Concorde, and the diesel trucks barrelling down the Boulevard St-Michel.

We have a saying in the private eye business—before turning to subtleties, do not forget the obvious. Therefore, I turned and redescended the carpeted stairs to the telephones, the toilets, and the tiresome concierge.

She frowned as I heaved into her line of vision, and I noticed her right hand moved to rest protectively on top of her precious towels. I nodded to her curtly—a man of affairs not to be disturbed with inanities about towels in telephone booths—and then realized that I had used up my only jeton on the previous call.

I had no time to fool around. I fished a hundred franc note out of my pocket. "Five jetons, *s'il vous plaît,* and keep the change."

This brought a smile to her parched and bloodless lips. My unorthodox behavior was backed by good French currency, so I was probably all right after all.

Clutching my coins, I rushed to the telephone booth. It was now occupied by a large blonde woman of middle years and considerable makeup, settled in for what looked like an all-day chat with her mother living in a garden apartment in Passy or St-Germain-en-Laye.

I tapped on the glass with my jeton, hoping to intimidate her. I had forgotten that I was in Paris, home of the Unflappables. She gave me a look that said, clear as clear, "Go back to your gutter and your bottle, miserable *sans-culotte.*" Then she turned back to the telephone, evidently determined to talk until the café closed or hell froze over, whichever came first.

In desperation I turned to the concierge, who had been watching this with the usual ironic smile.

"Madame," I said, "I need to make a call of an emergency nature. Can you help me?" As I spoke I did not neglect to put down on her desk yet another hundred franc note.

This brought about an immediate softening in her expression. "M'sieu is a doctor?" she enquired.

"Exactement!" I cried. A private detective is after all a sort of physician to ills within the body social. Or so I could argue if the need ever arose.

"Follow me, m'sieu." She rose from behind her desk, scooping up the coins in her dish and putting them into a pocket of her black bombazine dress. She led me through a door marked No Exit, down a corridor dimly lit with tiny light bulbs, to a door marked No Entry. She unlocked it, pushed it open, and entered, with me following close behind.

We were in a sort of storeroom. One wall was lined to the ceiling with steel shelving, upon which rested rows of glassware. There was a battered old desk in the middle of the room. Lying face down on the desk was a small balding man with his pants down around his ankles. I thought I had stumbled on yet another case of foul play when the man turned his head, revealing beneath him a smallish woman with elaborately curled hair and a dark skirt hiked up around her hips.

The ensuing argument between the three of them started at a shriek and built from there. I spotted the telephone and went for it, as the concierge explained that M'sieu le Docteur had to make a call of an emergency nature and why did not M'sieu Albert and Mamsel' Fifi seek out a cheap hotel for their coupling?

This time a receptionist answered Clovis' phone. Aware of the ears fastened on me, so to speak, I said, "Docteur Draconian here. I must speak to Monsieur Clovis immediately."

"But you are not M. Clovis' regular doctor," the receptionist said. "What has happened to Dr. d'Amboise?"

"Called away to surgery. I must speak to Clovis immediately."

"Is it anything to do with his test?"

"It could be," I said.

"Positive or negative?"

"I am at *liberté* to reveal that only to M. Clovis himself."

"You can tell me," she said. "M. Clovis keeps no secrets from me."

"Then he will tell you himself. But my instructions in these matters are clear. Mademoiselle, please do not waste any more of my time. Put me through to M. Clovis."

"Ah, I am desolated to have to tell you that M. Clovis has left instructions that no one is to be told where he is. In confidence, I can tell you that he is shooting the climactic scene of his new movie tonight. No one is allowed on the set except the actors and the technical people. But as soon as M. Clovis returns—"

"I don't think you understand," I said. "I am also appearing in the film."

It took her a moment to assimilate that. "You are M. Clovis' *docteur,* and you are also an actor?"

"Yes, of course. I play the part of the foreign *docteur.*"

She didn't like it. "If you're quite sure. . . ."

"Of course I'm sure! My presence is required on the set. Mademoiselle, there will be great disruptions if I do not appear."

After a few moments of dithering, she came to a decision. "Very well, I will tell you, but I hope it does not get me into difficulties. Tonight's shoot is to be held at La Closerie de Lilas on Montparnasse. Or rather, the cast will meet there first for dinner, then go on to the final location."

"Which is?"

"I do not myself know, m'sieu. M. Clovis intends to reveal that at the cast party."

I thanked her profusely and rung off. When I turned around I saw that the smallish balding man and the smallish woman with elaborately coiffed hair were no longer in *deshabille.* All neatly buttoned up now, they stood in a row with the concierge staring at me.

"Many thanks, madame," I said to the concierge, bowed to the other two, and started toward the door.

"One moment, m'sieu, if you please," said the man.

"Yes?" I said, slightly discomfitted by the intensity of their gaze. "We did not know you were an actor," the concierge said.

"I suppose not," I said, wondering if it were a crime to impersonate a film star.

"Would you mind giving us your autograph?" the man asked.

"With very great pleasure," I said.

The man produced a large menu. I scrawled my name across it and handed it to him.

He looked at it, puzzled, then said, "Perhaps m'sieu would also be good enough to honor us with his stage name?"

"But of course!" I took the menu again. Quickly, boldly, I scrawled across the top, impelled by the sort of fatal caprice that seems so logical in Paris, "Best regards from Alain Delon."

"I'm his stuntman," I explained before they could point out the lack of resemblance.

ON CAMERA 42

I MISSED THE party at the Closerie de Lilas, but, for a suitable tip, the maître d' remembered overhearing the instructions given to the taxis when Clovis' party was leaving. They had gone to the Hôtel Lauzan on the Île St-Louis. I took a taxi there.

The Île St-Louis is a small island in the Seine just above the Île de la Cité, almost at the geographic center of Paris. It is a refuge of small cobblestoned streets, silent quays and unpretentious architecture. The Hôtel Lauzan was once the residence of some of France's most famous poets and painters. Now owned and splendidly refurbished by the City of Paris, it forms a superb backdrop for historical dramas.

Right. So I walked in to a scene of people in powdered wigs making hissing remarks to each other under kleig lights. Spotting Clovis I made my way to him.

"Glad you got here," Clovis said. "You're playing Baudelaire in this scene."

"Really?" I said. "You really want me to play Baudelaire?"

I mean I was really flattered but I was having difficulty holding Clovis' attention because he had just seen an old friend across the room, a tall olive-skinned guy in a camel's-hair topcoat, maybe a French gangster, or an actor impersonating a French gangster, or even somebody entirely different impersonating an actor impersonating a French gangster, because they play these games in Paris, at least among the class able to afford several changes of clothing.

I turned to Yvette, who was standing by with her clipboard full of lists and scripts and lighting instructions. "Yes," she said. "It is a very great honor, even if it is a complicated joke on Clovis' part, part of his actor-trouvé method which is so controversial. Come with me to costuming; we'd better get you dressed and made up."

I followed her across the crowded little room. We went down a corridor and came to a door marked Wardrobe. Inside, Yvette told the wardrobe lady, whose name I never did catch, that I was Clovis's newest Baudelaire.

While the wardrobe lady went to get my costume, I said to Yvette, "What do you mean, his newest Baudelaire? How many has he had?"

"You're the third." She called out to the wardrobe lady, "Don't forget the Baudelaire shoes!"

"Which ones?" the wardrobe lady shouted back. "The striped dream sequence shoes or the dissolving-sanity black and gray shoes?"

"The black and grays."

I asked, "What happened to the other two Baudelaires?"

The wardrobe lady came back with a pile of heavy-looking dark clothing, a white shirt, and the black and gray shoes. Yvette motioned for me to gather everything up, then led me back into the corridor.

"The other two," I asked again. "What happened to them?"

"One of them was arrested for attempted bank robbery in Nice. He was, as you would imagine, a two-career man, though of course Clovis hadn't known that when he engaged him."

"And the other?"

"Victim of a hit-and-run. Two months in the hospital."

"The role hasn't had much luck. I wonder why Clovis picked me."

"Because you're the right size," Yvette said. "There's not time to run up new costumes. Especially the shoes, that's difficult on short notice."

"What's so special about the shoes?"

"Clovis has a theory about Charles Baudelaire and shoes. Shoes are Clovis' main symbol for the changes of temperament that Baudelaire underwent."

"Is this movie about Baudelaire?"

"Not exactly," Yvette said. "It's difficult to say what a Clovis movie is about. No one knows anything until Clovis finishes editing and reshooting and reshooting. You can change in there." She indicated a door.

"Yvette," I said, "I'm sorry I didn't keep our appointment the other day."

"It is of no concern," she said, in a manner which clearly indicated to me that it was. And I was pleased for a moment, because the fact that I had disturbed her implied that she felt something for me. But then on second thought, I realized that anyone would be annoyed at being stood up for dinner; it wasn't necessarily personal.

"Is anything the matter?" Yvette said.

"No, why do you ask?"

"Because you stood there for the longest time just looking at the ceiling, and I thought you were having an attack or something."

"Call it an illumination," I said. "Is it true that Alex is here?"

"Oh, yes. He's around somewhere."

"Did you tell him I was looking for him?"

"I haven't spoken to him today. But I assume that Monsieur Clovis has told him. You'd better start changing."

I opened the door and went into a little anteroom. Yvette came as far as the doorway. There was a screen in the far corner and I began changing behind it.

An uncanny feeling came over me, in the hot little dressing room, as I buttoned up my long black Baudelaire coat and stepped out to be fitted with moustache and makeup. Yvette was standing there looking casual and cute in her Lois jeans and white shirt top. Her dark hair was done up in a ponytail. There was a faint sheen of perspiration on her upper lip, a glow of color in her cheeks. She looked as fresh and vital as springtime itself, and then I cut it off because I really didn't know what disaster my fatal mentality was setting me up for this time.

"I'd like to see you when this case is finished," I told her.

She gave me a nice smile, a smile that could have meant anything, the sort of smile you give when everything is wide open and the world looks hopeful.

And then Clovis was calling her from the corridor, and Yvette came up to me and pressed something hairy into my hand.

"Here is your moustache," she said. *"Bon chance."*

HÔTEL LAUZAN 43

THE HÔTEL LAUZAN is located on the Quai d'Anjou on the north side of the Île St-Louis, almost equidistant between the Pont Marie and the Pont de Sully. I used to live there when I was Baudelaire, in a little room under the eaves. From there I watched the Seine stretch and preen itself, and found, in the contrast between the river's protean mutability and the fixed lines of the quays and bridges, a symbol for art itself. That was quite a while ago, before the unfortunate matter with Jeane Duval.

Still, that was a few years ago, and now, since I was enjoying one of my increasingly rare fits of sanity, I had decided to take myself back there again. Tonight was the regular meeting of the Club des Haschischiens, the famous Hashish Club where so many notables assembled, not all approving, of course, but fascinated by our custom, anxious to talk to us, peering in wonder at our effrontery, eager to worship at the shrine of our intelligence.

I wrapped my long cloak more closely around me: it was a bitter night. I stroked my rather striking moustache, and I entered the hotel.

The camera tracked me to the stairs. Our leader, La Présidente, as we call her, was there to greet me. I went past her, climbed the stairs and went to the cramped east room. The air was dense with smoke from the charcoal fire and the candles, and from the pipes of the tophatted gentlemen. They sat on sofas, or lounged in easy chairs covered with figured silks and satins, long slender pipes in their mouths, talking, laughing, arguing between puffs. As I watched, they seemed to waver ever so slightly, as though they were becoming the hallucinations they sought.

I spotted my dear friend Théophile Gautier, somewhat taller than I had expected. *"Ca va?"* I enquire of him.

"Oh, the party's just warming up," he replied. "The usual crowd is here, as you can see—Delacroix on that couch, Boissard with the silly hat on his head, the Goncourt brothers looking supercilious as always."

"Who's that fat fellow with the coffee cup?"

"M. Balzac. He comes only for the conversation, since he claims that his consumption of coffee and spirits renders him immune to the effects of the Black Smoke."

From the corner of my eye, through a haze of lights, I could see Clovis making circular motions with his arms. I interpreted that as meaning that he wanted Gautier and me to walk around, so the camera could track us. I took hold of Gautier's arm and led him slowly across the room.

"And who are those two over there?" I asked, because two men had just entered and were looking with stern eyes upon the proceedings.

"The one on the left is Wagner, of course; you can tell by his floppy tie. The other is an up-and-coming young poet named Rilke."

Wagner and Rilke walked over to us. The cameras turned to them. I said to Gautier, under my breath, "Alex, that *is* you under the beard, isn't it?"

"That would be telling," Gautier said. "How in hell are you, Hob?"

"Me? I'm fine. But how the hell are you? And what in hell are you up to?"

"We'll talk later," Alex said. "Frankly, old buddy, I am really glad to see you."

44 WRAP-UP; MOULES WITH ALEX

CLOVIS WRAPPED IT up soon after that. Below, a reception room had been set aside for the cast party that was one of Clovis' signatures. I removed my costume and my makeup. Already I was coming down a little from the privilege of having been Charles Baudelaire. But, I reminded myself, it's not so terrible to be good old Hob Draconian, especially when he is on the verge of solving his case.

I had expected Alex to give me the slip again. It would be in keeping with everything else that had happened so far. But that wasn't what happened at all. He sought me out at the cast party and suggested that we slip away and get a drink somewhere and talk. We left the party and took a taxi. Alex knew a student place near the Panthéon, and we went there. I don't remember what it was called. Le Moule Dorade, I suppose, since everything in Paris is at least gilded if not golden.

There was a tiny spotlit platform and on it people were dancing very slowly to the sound of drum machine, electric guitar and swizzle stick. They moved so slowly. This was the thing to do, control freaks were in, the old willpower thing, we've all seen it before now. It wears this year's clothes and it probably has something to do with why anyone would be interested in Clovis' cockamamie ideas about Baudelaire's shoes. His imputation of importance to the notion irritated me. What did he think he was, weird poseur with his zeitgeist all pat, coming on with his pronunciamentos ex cathedra?

The band was about what you'd expect in a chichi place like this, mandolin and wooden flute playing folksongs of Brittany. We ordered a pitcher of beet-red Belgian beer, a plate of mussels in a spicy marinara sauce, and fell to.

Alex hadn't changed much in the ten years since I'd seen him. He was tall, muscular, blond, good looking. He seemed ill at ease, however, and had chosen our table carefully, sitting with his back to the wall so that he could see everyone who came in or out.

"So what's new?" Alex asked.

I shrugged. "What should be new? I'm a private detective now. I guess that's new."

"Quite a change from the old days," Alex said. "Do you ever play poker any more?"

"Rarely."

"How's the detective business coming along?"

"Not bad. I found you."

"Yes, so you did. But that doesn't count. I was trying to get in touch with you, as a matter of fact."

"Were you? What for?"

"Hob, I need some help. I'm willing to pay for it, too."

"What's the trouble?"

Alex's story began some years back. He had left Europe, just as I had, returned to the States and began looking for work. He had passed his bar exam in Washington, D.C., some years before. Now, with the help of one of his uncles, he went to work for the Selwyn Corporation, a group of fund-raisers. This was in 1985. By 1986 Alex found himself in the middle of an interesting situation, raising money for the Contras, and for the secret Iran initiative that the White House was promulgating during those years. Although "Spitz" Chanell was the one who would get into the news for his fund-raising activities, Selwyn and others were also active.

This was also the time when Alex met Rachel. She was one of the secretaries working for Selwyn. She and Alex began to go out together. Within a month they had moved into a little Georgetown apartment. Alex went on working for Selwyn.

Over the next months, Alex couldn't help but notice that a lot of money was being raised for various initiatives concerning the Contras and Iran. But as much as came in, little of it ever seemed to get to the combatants. It was a curious situation. Everything was being done in terms of patriotism, but some people seemed to be making a lot of money out of it.

Then came 1987 and suddenly Iran and the Contras were in the news. They were linked, Iran-Contra, also known as Irangate. Casey went in for his brain operation and never returned to full health, dying soon after. Colonel Oliver North was fired. Admiral Poindexter, his superior, was in trouble. A lot of people were going to be in trouble before this one was finished.

Alex could see that his days in this job were numbered. In fact, the days of Selwyn, Ltd., were also numbered.

It was then in those final days that Alex saw the handwriting on the wall. It took a little time for it to sink in that his superiors had been engaged in something that, no matter how it looked when they began, looked illegal as hell now.

The net of the investigations was thrown wide, and a lot of little fish were being pulled in. Politics being what it was, you could be sure that a lot more little fish were going to get jail sentences than the big fish. And Alex was not in a good spot. Because, however innocently, he was involved.

Selwyn had learned of his Swiss account and had taken advantage of it from time to time, as a transfer point for contributions for the Contras, or for whoever was getting them. There was no profit in this for Alex, but it looked like he was going to get into plenty of trouble.

He discussed it with Rachel. She had learned, along the secretarial grapevine, that investigators from the Special Prosecutor's office were going to start checking into his dealings with Selwyn.

"It wasn't so much that I couldn't prove my innocence," Alex said. "I could, though it would have taken time and money. The main thing was, I'd have had to stay in Washington while the thing dragged on. I couldn't do that. You know me, Hob."

I nodded. I couldn't have stood for that, myself; not if there were any other way out. "So what did you do?"

"I figured it was time to pack up and get going. In fact, it looked almost too late. Rachel had heard that there was a subpoena out for me. I left that same evening. Rachel stayed behind to take care of final details, get rid of the apartment, put stuff into storage, all that sort of thing. And then she was supposed to meet me in Paris."

"That part of it I know," I said. "But then you disappeared. Or so Rachel said."

"Yes, I did, didn't I?" Alex said, an amused smile on his face. "Or I seemed to, at any rate. As far as Rachel was concerned, I had disappeared. That, of course, was when she hired you."

I nodded. "What actually happened?"

"I ducked out of sight for a while," Alex said. "It seemed a good idea at the time. I'd heard something about Rachel which disturbed me."

"What was that?"

"It seemed she was talking to one of the special investigators. A guy named Romagna. Maybe you've seen him around?"

I nodded. "He's around. But why would Rachel do that?"

Alex gave me a long, somber look. "You've seen her Damascene routine?"

"Yeah, when she came into my office the first time."

"She does weird things sometimes, Rachel. She's a Mormon, you know. They raise some strange ones. You never know when she's going to get an idea that she has to do something. She's probably OK; maybe I was just paranoid, but I thought I'd better get out to Europe."

"What about Romagna?"

"I don't know if he has a warrant for me or not. But he's hanging in a little too tight for my peace of mind. I thought I'd stay out of things for a while and see what was up."

"Have you seen enough now?"

"Yes, I think so. My mind's made up now. I'm ready for the next step."

"And what will that be?"

"That's the part I need your help for," Alex said.

"No," I said.

"Hob, just listen to me."

Same old Alex. And I was listening to him. Same old Hob.

10

LA BAULE 45

Please do not ask me to explain how Alex got me from a taverna in the center of Paris eating *moules* and drinking wine to the passenger side of a rented Citroën speeding through the dark Paris countryside with the glow of the city behind us and the Atlantic coast ahead. I must have been crazy. Alex has that effect on me. There's no buddy like a good old buddy. And, like some other men who have had multiple wives and replaceable families, don't ask which means more to me, family or friends.

And I felt more than a little guilty, because here I was, flying through the night with Alex, like we had done so many times before, and I was laughing at his jokes like I used to do, and we were both a little drunk and the countryside was dark, vast, empty, mysterious, and we the only humans as far as the eye could see, Alex and me under the stars of Mother Night. So I'm sentimental; shoot me.

At least I was able to convince myself, not without reason, that I was actually doing my job, following Alex to wherever it was he was going, so that I could report to Rachel, my employer (who might be in cahoots with Romagna) Alex's whereabouts. Of course, I'd also tell Alex exactly what I was going to do, so he could take his precautions, but what the hell, there's nothing in my client's agreement that says I have to do in an old buddy.

Alex had said he'd explain, and I allowed him to pull me out of the security of the taverna near the Panthéon with its long wooden benches full of French college students, its pitchers of beer, cheerful, sweaty, shirtsleeved waiters, the plates of mussel shells—blue-black, nacre.

At least I could give myself the illusion I was still doing it for Rachel, my employer, flying out into the night like this with Alex in order to learn his whereabouts, after which I would report to Rachel and she, perhaps, would report to Romagna. Only I would previously have told Alex I was going to tell her.

Well, maybe I didn't know what in hell I thought. His rented Citroën convertible had a blown muffler and I couldn't even hear myself think, much less talk with Alex about what was going on. He'd probably kicked a hole in the muffler himself in order not to have to talk to me. Nobody tells me anything. But even for me, enough is enough.

"Alex," I said.

"What is it, buddy?"

"Stop the car somewhere, OK?"

"What's up?"

"We need to talk."

He looked at me. I looked back at him. He understood.

"OK, buddy," he said, "as a matter of fact, there's a nice little restaurant not far from here, right close to Angers. We need a break."

He was doing what I'd asked, but he was giving nothing away. I'd always admired Alex. Which didn't necessarily mean I'd do what he wanted.

I remembered only later that Alex had a positive affinity for the world's worst eating places. I wish I'd thought of that and eaten some more mussels in Paris before we turned into the parking lot of the dark little inn on the N23 just south of Le Mans.

It was one of those thatch-roof affairs that always should be viewed with suspicion, and it turned out to be an overpriced bad eatery, something rare in France, but trust Alex to find the exception.

All right, I'm exaggerating; maybe it wasn't that bad, but I had suddenly remembered that I hadn't had a decent meal since I'd come to Paris and to be frank, I was feeling more than a little churlish about it. Wouldn't you?

It may seem like an odd place to begin complaining, in the middle of a mad dash to the French seacoast, to La Baule, to be precise, located a few miles past the not-very-famous port (except to Second World War German-submarine buffs) of St-Nazaire. But there it is; I complain when I please. And even though I had agreed to help Alex, due apparently to some blind impulse powered by déjà vu, I was now having second thoughts, to say nothing of third and fourth thoughts, and indeed all thoughts up to and beyond the transfinite series.

Over cups of dismal coffee, but with an acceptable cognac to accompany them, I asked Alex to explain just what the hell he was doing now and why he found it necessary to have me along.

"It's very simple," Alex said. "I've got to disappear."

"You already did that, remember?"

"That time was just playing around. This time's for good."

"What are you talking about?"

"Hob, they've got me boxed. The people I work for. I finally got the angle. They're going to put it on me."

"What are you talking about?"

"The whole Iran-Contra missing funds business."

"How can they do that?"

"They're going to claim that I scammed them, diverted key funds to my own account. I should never have let them use my account. I thought I was so smart. Anyhow, I'm going to step out of the world for a few years, give it all a chance to settle down."

"Step out? Where? How?"

"The old identity trick."

"A new passport?"

"A total set of papers. An entire personality I can step into. These people I'm going to meet can arrange it."

"Is that where we're going? To meet some forgers?"

"It's safe," Alex said, "but I'm a little nervous about them all the same. That's why I need you to back me up."

"Why bother dealing with these guys at all? If you really need a forger, I'll find you one in Paris."

"These guys produce first-class documentation. And they have just what I need. It'll go all right. Especially when they see I'm not alone."

I fell silent and couldn't help but think, cynically, that if Alex were relying on me for when the shooting started, he didn't know how alone he was. I don't know what he thought private detectives do, but a lot of us get along nicely without guns, boring as that may sound.

"You mean you're not armed?"

"Certainly not. What do you take me for? Some sort of a thug?"

Alex shook his head and took something out of his pocket and tapped my knee with it. It was solid and metallic. The thing, not my knee.

"What are you doing?" I asked with some irritation.

"Take it," Alex said. "Put it in your pocket."

I reached under the table. He put a large, slightly oily automatic into my hand.

"Now just a minute," I said.

"Hob, you won't have to actually use it."

"Damn right I won't have to use it. I'm not taking it. Here, take it back."

I reached with it under the table.

"Hob," he pleaded, "please don't make a scene."

"Damn it," I said, "take back the piece."

"Hob, listen—"

"No, you listen; take back the goddamned piece."

"I'm trying to tell you I'll pay you two thousand dollars just to keep the gun in your pocket."

"Two thousand dollars?" I said.

"That's what I said."

"But not to use it?"

"Just to hold on to it and show it, if necessary."

"Two thousand dollars?" I asked.

He nodded.

"It's easy to say," I told him.

"Hold out your hand under the table," he said.

"Just a minute," I said. "I have to put this thing away." I managed to stuff the bulky automatic into a jacket pocket, where it made an unsightly bulge and probably left an indelible stain. Then I reached under the table again.

"Check this out," Alex said, and put something in my hand.

It was an envelope.

The envelope was filled with something.

About half an inch of something.

I peeked. Lovely thousand franc French notes. I riffled them. They'd probably come to two thousand dollars American close enough. I put them into my pocket.

"Let me explain the ground rules," I said. "First of all, I'm not going to shoot anyone. I don't know what you've read about private detectives, but we don't do that."

"Don't worry," Alex said. "The gun's just for show."

"Isn't it loaded?"

"Of course."

"Why, if it's just for show?"

"It's not possible to bluff properly with an unloaded gun. Come on, Hob, let's get out of here."

We paid up and piled out into Alex's Citroën. Then we were off down the dark road, proceeding at speed through low, flat country with high hedges on either side.

"What's our next stop?" I asked.

"Angers."

We were in the heart of nothing, and we were on our way to nowhere. The auspices were terrible. But I did have an unanticipated two thousand dollars.

THE HIT 46

We went through Angers around midnight. The streets were without sidewalks, the buildings lining the streets shoulder to shoulder. High, narrow buildings with steep eaves. A tangle of stone streets like the petrified entrails of a medieval monster. Europe is our past, we must go back from time to time to exhume it psychically, penetrate the layers that lead to our guts. Grays and browns, and sometimes a glint of starlight.

But then, just a few hundred yards within the sleeping city, we saw the right-hand turn marked Nantes-Rennes-Laval. We took it through the suburbs and followed it through small towns near the banks of the Loire: St-Georges-sur-Loire, Varades, Ancenis, coming at last to Nantes. There was no time to stop and sample the frogs' legs, a speciality of the region. We continued watching the signs for Vannes and Rennes. We followed them onto a dual carriage road, through a lot of construction, emerging at last on the N165. We continued through open countryside for fifteen miles, then, just before Savenay, turned onto N171. Soon we were rolling through the dark industrial heart of St-Nazaire, and past it to the little town of La Baule, just a few miles past St-Nazaire.

It was going on 4:00 A.M. We followed a road along the coast, passed through La Baule itself, a huddle of Breton houses, and came to a group of docks situated just beyond the mouth of the Loire, but sheltered from the open Atlantic by a curving headland to the north.

Alex parked the car close to the docks. He turned to me. "Do you know how to use that gun?"

I took it out of my pocket and examined it by Alex's small penlight. It was a Browning .45 calibre automatic. I couldn't quite remember how the safeties worked. As I've mentioned, firearms are not my thing and I manage most of the time to do well enough without them. Alex watched me fumble for a moment or two then took it out of my hand.

"Like this," he said, extracting the clip and ejecting the round in the chamber. He showed me how to put the clip back in, jack a cartridge into the barrel, and how to operate the safeties. Finally, he handed it back to me, the hammer set on half cock.

"All the safeties are off except the half cock," he said. "To shoot, just thumb the hammer down. Then point, aim and squeeze. Nothing to it."

"Since I'm not going to shoot anyone," I said, "I really don't have to know all that stuff."

"Hob, as a private detective you are a disaster. Look, I'm paying you two thousand dollars just to look dangerous. Or at least competent. The least you can do in return is pay attention when I show you how the thing works."

"All right," I said grudgingly. I took the automatic again and went through the moves. After all, since I *was* in the detective business, you could never tell when this sort of thing might come in useful.

"Ready?" Alex said after a few minutes.

"Sure, I'm ready," I told him. To be perfectly frank, I was feeling less than unmitigated enthusiasm. But the two thousand dollars in French notes did a lot for my motivation. Also, I had always liked Alex and this was a chance to help him out.

We left the car and walked along the dockside. About twenty yards down, Alex identified the rendezvous: a pier belonging to Dupont et Fils, Shippers. The high iron gate had been left unlocked, so we were able to go through it and around the main building to the wharves on the other side.

We walked until we came to a long pier extending out into the water. There was a bright light at the end of it, and Alex indicated that this was the place where the exchange was to take place.

"Hob," he said, "I want you to stay back here. Just make sure no one else comes out onto the pier."

"What do I do if they try anyhow?"

"Just tell them to go away."

I didn't like it, but what was there to do? I found a tall iron diesel barrel to crouch behind. Alex drew a small revolver out of his pocket, a .32, I suppose, checked the chambers, looked at me, said, "Wish me luck, old buddy," and started down the pier.

Even before Alex walked out on the dock, I could hear the low throbbing of a boat's engine in the harbor, closing on the pier. As he walked to the end, I could make out the boat's shape, a darker mass against the medium gray darkness of the sky and water. The shadow of the boat crept up to the pier without lights. I could see Alex standing at the end, in silhouette.

The boat nudged the pier with a creak. I took out the .45 and set it on full cock. I still wasn't planning to use it, but no sense in being careless.

Two men climbed up onto the pier. I could see them in silhouette, short men who contrasted sharply with Alex's tall figure. Then I heard a noise behind me.

I turned, the Browning in my hand, but I couldn't see a thing. When I turned back, I saw that there were three men on the dock now, all of them shorter than Alex. They had started to argue. I couldn't make out what was being said, but it was getting louder, and one of the men was swearing.

Then there was a scuffle. Alex pulled free, and I heard the sound of a revolver going off. One of the men staggered back, clutching his arm and cursing. After that things happened very quickly. Alex whirled around, and I heard shots fired. I had the impression that Alex was firing his handgun. Then I heard the sound of an automatic weapon, an ugly sound in the night. Alex's hat flew into the air and I saw his head explode as a tracer went into it.

Alex's body tumbled down onto the pier. The men on the pier gathered it up and lowered it into the boat. The boat took off.

I stood there for what felt like a very long time, the loaded gun in my hand, looking out to sea.

FAUCHON 47

I CAN'T REMEMBER how I got back to Paris. Presumably I drove Alex's car. I just couldn't remember doing it. A lot of me was on automatic, just doing what had to be done. I couldn't even remember where I parked the car. There was a blank of some hours. Then I found myself in a café on the Champs-Élysées having a cognac. Whenever I tried to think what happened, my mind winced away from it. If I pursued it, it showed me images: the dark pier, the lighter gray of the water, the people in silhouette, the flash of the handguns, and then the brilliant tracer fingers of the automatic weapon. Then Alex falling back, his head blown open. . . .

I don't remember how I got from the bar in the Champs-Élysées to Fauchon's office. I was preoccupied with fatigue and guilt, the feeling that somehow I was responsible.

I told Fauchon what I had seen. He heard me out without a change of expression. Not a raised eyebrow, not even a little quirk to the mouth. He was a solid man, Fauchon, and he hunched there in his straightbacked wooden chair and jotted down notes in his little black pocket notebook.

When I was finished he asked me if I had anything more to add. I said that I didn't. He excused himself and went to a desk in the back of the room. He made a phone call, talked with someone for a while, then came back to me.

"I spoke to the gendarmerie in St-Nazaire," he told me. "They have no report of disturbances last night in La Baule. They'll check out the area and call me back. Are you sure you haven't left out anything?"

"That's it," I told him. "You don't seem too impressed. I suppose it wasn't a very interesting murder."

"So far," he told me, "we have only your word that a murder was committed at all."

I stared at him. I found his attitude difficult to believe. "You mean you won't take my word for it?"

"I do not think you are trying to lie to me," Fauchon said. "But I have noted that you are an emotional man, and probably given to hallucinations from time to time. You are the visionary type so aptly described by Jung. And you have been under considerable strain recently."

"Psychoanalysis is just what I need," I said, my voice heavy with sarcasm and self-pity. "Do you have any other insights for me?"

"Just that you get into some ridiculous situations for the sake of friendship."

"Maybe I do," I said. "Meanwhile, what do I do now?"

"I would like you to remain in Paris for the next few days. If we find any evidence pointing to a crime, we will want to interview you further."

ROMAGNA 48

What I needed was an American sort of place where I could tie on an American-style drunk, starting with margaritas and nachos and ending with vomiting in the bathroom. I knew just the place. A taxi took me to Le Cowboy, a Tex-Mex restaurant on a second floor in the Place du 18 Juin 1940 right across from the Montparnasse railroad station. Le Cowboy was your basic southwestern transplant. It had a map of the Republic of Texas on one wall, a Mexican poncho on another. There were Spanish tiles on the floor and the waitresses wore short cheerleader skirts and cowboy boots.

I sat down at the bar but before I could get decently started on Project Blotto, Romagna found me. I told him about Alex. Like Fauchon, he seemed neither surprised, regretful, nor entirely believing.

"So he's finally gone, is he?" That was Romagna's epitaph for Alex.

I nodded.

"But Fauchon hasn't found any evidence?"

"Not yet."

"Then perhaps we shouldn't count him out yet."

He sat there at the bar beside me, a large clumsy man hunched over a stein of beer. "Are you by any chance with the Special Prosecutor's office?" I asked him.

He smiled. "That's right."

"And you're here to take Alex back?"

Romagna shook his head. "It's U.S. Marshalls who do that. I'm here on other business. But it was convenient to keep an eye on Alex, too."

"Why don't you go after the big boys and leave Alex alone?"

"Innocent little Alex," Romagna sneered.

I don't like it when other people are sarcastic. I'm the one who does that. Romagna's expression seemed to betray smug knowledge that I was not privy to.

Romagna took a pull at his beer and said, "Alex told you his account was being used by Selwyn?"

I nodded.

"Care to hear a different version?"

"All right," I said.

"Let's get a table and order a pitcher of margaritas," Romagna said. "Do you mind if I smoke a cigar?"

It was the last day of the operation. Alex and Selwyn had been cooking the books all day. The bank accounts were a mess. Little wonder, since Selwyn had been cutting into the accounts heavily, juggling millions into accounts he controlled abroad.

By four in the afternoon they had done what they could. It wasn't good enough. Selwyn knew it.

"I'm in a poor position," he told Alex. "The Feds are going to try to tag me for any money that's unaccounted for. But the fact is, I actually kept very little of it. The funds were disbursed into other accounts that I have no access to."

"If it comes to it," Alex said, "you can probably make a deal."

"It really wouldn't be wise," Selwyn said. "At the worst I'm going to have to do a few years. Time off for good behavior. But when I get out I'll be all right. I've kept faith with my people and they'll keep faith with me."

"Amen to that, brother," Alex said. "As for me, I'm leaving the country for a while. Settle down in Paris and write my memoirs."

"I've got a family; I can't do that," Selwyn said, a little wistfully. "Well, this is the last of it." He took out a large blue check and handed it to Alex.

"From our Persian Gulf friends. Put it in the Arabco Account."

The check was for ten million dollars, the largest single contribution received. Alex put it in his briefcase and took a last look through his desk. He had emptied it out the previous day. He picked up his briefcase and started for the door.

Alice Mills at the front reception desk smiled at him sardonically. "Off to the fleshpots of Europe, eh?"

Alex smiled. He had had Alice book the flight for him. She'd been mentioning it ever since, hinting not so subtly that she might be induced into going along.

Alex didn't figure she was what he needed at all. He waved goodbye to her and went out the door.

He took a taxi down to the First National on State and Pine. Alex, as Selwyn's boy of all legal and semilegal chores, had been authorized as a signatory to contribution checks. It was easier for Selwyn, who spent most of his time with clients and contributors, to let Alex do the shifting and moving of the funds from one account to another.

Alex stood in front of the bank. He'd never thought of it as money before. Not while the excitement of the Iran arms dealings was on, not while they were diverting funds to the Contras. It had been cops and robbers on the highest level, and he'd had a lot of fun. He also had to admit that he hadn't thought the position through to its conclusion. This sudden breakup of the Selwyn Corporation, the congressional investigation, the whole thing should have been predictable somewhere along the line. Yes, it had bothered him, but he'd thought the guys he worked for knew what they were doing. The stakes were so big, the operation so well protected, it was difficult to conceive that the whole thing had come unstuck.

Well, that's what had happened, and here he was with the last check. One more to funnel into the network. . . .

But what if he didn't do that? What if he kept it for himself?

He'd never been a big grifter, just small time. But here he was with a check for ten million bucks. He knew just how to whip that in and out of his Swiss account to the safety of a supplementary numbered account he had set up in Liechtenstein.

The big boys had been caught with their hands in the till. Now was the time for the employees to rip off what was left.

He had his passport in the briefcase with him. He didn't bother to return to his apartment for his clothing. When you get someone else's ten million in your pocket, it's time to move. He flew out of Dulles that evening, first class on Air France.

"That's your theory," I told him.

"It doesn't matter a rat's ass to me any more," Romagna said. "I've been pulled off the case. I'm going home tonight. But not because I believe Alex is dead. I think he staged the whole thing."

"But why?"

"So you could be witness to his death. His supposed death. Once that was accepted by the authorities, he was off the hook, really safe in his new identity, and able to spend his ten million anywhere he pleased."

"What ten million? You must be talking about one of the principals in this Iran-Contra thing."

"No, I'm talking about Alex. Him and that secretary of his, that Rachel Starr. I'm pretty sure she put Alex up to it. And now she's over here to collect her share of the money. This little death or whatever it is of Alex's is going to put a crimp in her plans, I imagine. But I can understand it from Alex's point of view: arrange a death and keep a few extra millions."

"Alex wouldn't do that," I said, almost automatically.

"He wouldn't?" Romagna said, suddenly turning vicious. "What do you know about him? All you know is he's your old buddy from the hippie days in Ibiza. We have a file on you, too. You're negligible. You're living in a dreamworld, and if you think Alex stayed the same barefoot boy you knew in Ibiza, you're really crazy."

"Can you prove it, about the ten million dollars?"

"No, we can't. Not yet, anyhow. But we're pretty sure."

I put down a bill for the drinks. "Have a nice journey home," I said, standing up.

"I guess this'll change things for Nieves, too," Romagna remarked.

I stopped with my hand on the doorknob. "Who is Nieves?"

"You think you know your old buddy so well. And you don't even know Nieves." He chuckled. "Go check it out, Mr. Private Investigator."

NIEVES 49

The lady was waiting for me in the lobby.

She rose when I came in, and I suppose Alex must have shown her a photograph of me because she had no trouble recognizing me. She was a slim and beautiful young woman with that look of class that comes from being born with a lot of money. Yes, and from something innate, too, to be fair about it. Black silk skirt, raw silk blouse, needle-pointed high heels. Anyhow, I would have bet everything I had that her first name was Nieves. And of course I won, though I didn't really get anything out of it.

"Mr. Draconian? I am Nieves Teresa Maria Sanchez y Issássaga. I need to talk to you badly."

"I guess we both need to talk," I said. "Shall we go to a café?"

"Your room would be better," she said. "My Air France flight was full, and I am tired and would like to take off my shoes."

So we went to my hotel room.

Nieves took the seat in the bay window and I sat on the padded wing chair. She sat very erect, one of those things they must teach them in Latin Princess Finishing School. Her hair was as shiny as a freshly groomed raven's wing. She wore a little gold cross around her neck. A braided gold bracelet. No lipstick, but her large, pouty, well-shaped lips had natural color. She also had on a little green eye shadow.

"Alex talked about you," she said. "You were his friend in the old days, in Spain."

"In Ibiza," I corrected her.

"Yes. It's like a club, isn't it?"

I nodded. "Where did you know Alex from?"

"Washington," she said. "I don't think you knew that we were to be married."

"No, I didn't know that."

We sat quietly for a while. I didn't know what in hell to say. Her fiancé had just been killed; what was there to say? I hoped she didn't want to hear the details again. I was getting sick of it, sick of Alex and his life and his death, sick of this stupid case which was beginning to depress me unutterably.

"Well," she said at last, "I want to tell you about it. I need some advice."

She'd picked a fine one to ask. Still, what can you say?

"Go ahead, I'm all ears," I said. And a small voice inside my head said, donkey ears, old boy, donkey ears.

ALEX, NIEVES 50

Alex met Nieves two years previously at an embassy ball, a reception at the Paraguayan Embassy. Alex loved to put on his silk tuxedo, slick back his hair, go to those affairs. It didn't matter that they were invariably dull. What Alex liked was the pomp and circumstance, the exquisitely decorated surroundings, the self-confident and strong-featured people who attended these events. Maybe it was fantasy, but Alex had had enough of realism. You get to see a lot of realism growing up in the Bronx. Alex liked pageantry much more than he liked real life, assuming that dirt and pain and shoddiness are real life.

He was having his usual good time at a party when he ran into Nieves. She was twenty-two years old and this was her first year in Washington. Her father was the new Assistant Cultural Attaché from Paraguay. She spoke almost perfect English, as well as French and German. She'd been trained to it from earliest years. She was cultured but provincial, awestruck by the world of Washington, so different from, yet so similar to, the closed little diplomatic world of Asunción.

Alex asked her to dance. They looked well together: Alex, tall, broad shouldered, blond; Nieves, small, with sleek black hair and a madonna's face.

Alex was about thirty-two at this time. Their affair began soon after. They were crazy about each other. But there were difficulties.

The big problem was social. Alex was a junior lawyer in Selwyn, Inc., a fund-raising firm in Washington, D.C. He didn't look like he was going anywhere important. He had no prospects. He could always make twenty or thirty thousand a year, maybe even get up to fifty grand. But he still was a long way from the money he'd need to live like Nieves' friends and relatives.

Nieves didn't like these problems. She played with the idea of marrying Alex anyhow. In time, her family would come around.

But Alex didn't want to do it that way. He agreed with Nieves' family that he was unworthy of her. Alex sincerely believed that wealth meant special privilege, special cachet. He was not cynical about wealth. He felt that as a poor boy—relatively—he had no right to marry into the monied class.

Of course, there was a good chance that Nieves' family would come around, and Nieves had quite a lot of money of her own. But this didn't suit Alex. He didn't want to live on his wife's money. He didn't see himself as a ponce. What was a dream for Jean-Claude—marrying a wealthy woman—was a nightmare for Alex.

He didn't want to live on his wife's money. He wanted money of his own. Alex was used to taking, not to being given.

This might have all stayed theoretical if Alex hadn't found himself in a position to make a coup. As one of the signatories to the bank accounts at Selwyn, Inc., he moved the contributions from one account to another, into still other accounts. It was difficult to tell who was getting what. That was the idea. But it seemed that the Contras weren't getting a whole lot of it.

A lot of the money was rubbing off, into accounts run by Selwyn and others. It was a scam. Alex began to look into how he could take some off himself—just as a theoretical exercise, at least at first.

It seemed easy enough. He could endorse a check into one of the Swiss accounts to which he was a signatory, then transfer the money into Alex's own Swiss account. Then transfer it from there into another account. It wouldn't even have his name on it. Just his number.

The idea began to intrigue him. Drop out and start all over again, but with a lot of money. Start a new life as a rich man with a beautiful wife in complaisant, corrupt Asunción.

He figured he could siphon off at least a hundred thousand dollars. Maybe more. In the general confusion and covering up, they'd probably be a long time getting around to him. By the time they did, he'd be long gone, and the money would simply have to be marked down as "unaccounted for," as happens so often in affairs of these sorts.

Rachel was a part of all this. Maybe the final ignition that set the idea in motion came from her. They had lived together for just over six months. There had never been any talk of love. Alex didn't love her, but he suspected, or feared, that she loved him.

Rachel had good ideas. She was a necessary part of the plan. There was no way to do it without having her in on it.

Alex discussed the whole thing with Nieves. She was a very level-headed girl, and a very passionate one. Unusual combination.

"I would live with you anyhow," she said. "Even if you had no money. I love you; that's all that matters. But I do like my life back home. And you would like it too, Alex. And I don't think you would be happy living on my money."

"No," Alex said.

"That is silly, but I respect you for it. It is a matter of pride with you. But it means you must get money of your own; otherwise you'll never be happy."

"Suppose I could get quite a lot of money," Alex said. "For the moment, never mind how. Would you marry me and live with me in Asunción?"

"Yes."

"Even if I had a different name and slightly altered appearance?"

"What are you talking about?"

Alex told her about Iran and the Contras, the contributions, and how he was thinking of tapping them rather heavily.

Nieves listened until he was finished, then laughed. "You had me scared for a moment. I thought you were thinking of robbing a bank or maybe a Seven-Eleven store. But what you're talking about doing, Alex darling, doesn't really qualify as a crime at all. You're going to relieve the thieves of a little of their loot. They should give you a medal."

"They could give me one hell of a long jail sentence if they caught me."

"Then if you're going to do it," Nieves said, "you'd better steal a lot, because you're just going to do it once and the sentence is probably the same, whether you take a lot or a little, if you get caught. But Alex, you mustn't get caught."

"I wasn't really planning to. I'm going to need Rachel's help on this one. She's in on it anyhow. I need her help, and I need to give her some of the profits."

"That's up to you, of course."

"We'll have to keep this quiet. No one must know about us. Not until I can marry you."

"I hope that won't take too long."

"Less than a month. I'm going to need the help of some of your friends. Can you give me some contacts in Paraguay?"

"Of course."

Then Alex had a moment of doubt. "Some people in Asunción may figure out who I am. Any problem?"

"Certainly not. They'll think it was clever of you. No one would tell the American authorities."

"Maybe a Paraguayan wouldn't tell. But an American might."

"Not our American friends in Asunción."

"What if one of them is the wrong kind of American?"

"Don't worry, my love. The wrong kind of American doesn't stay long in Paraguay."

Nieves opened her purse and found a tortoiseshell cigarette case. She lit up a long, dark brown Nat Sherman cigarette.

"Alex never told me his plans in so many words," Nieves

said. "The idea was, he would do what he had to do, and we would meet in Asunción. He wanted the names of some Paraguayans in Paris whom he could rely on. I had several friends there. You must understand, I didn't really know what was going on. I didn't really think it was so bad, taking money from those pompous fools who support these soldier-of-fortune causes. All I thought about was how Alex was going to come to me in Paraguay. He would look different. A moustache, at least. Maybe a little facial surgery. It was the most exciting thing I've ever been involved with. It was very romantic. And I was very much in love. Or very much infatuated. I guess that's why I didn't think it through until now."

"What did you think through now?"

"Well, what Alex would actually do. Take the money, of course. Go to Paris. Then disappear. Rachel would hire you to find him. That had all been planned beforehand. You were selected because you knew Alex well, and because Alex thought you would be . . . flexible."

"Flexible," I said bitterly. "You mean malleable. And gullible, to boot."

"It's a nice quality, Hob," she said. "Don't lose it."

"What else did you know?"

"You would witness Alex's death. He would be able to start a new life under an assumed name, with me, in Paraguay. But of course, there was one part that had been left out, one thing left that wasn't safe, one thing that was a loose end."

"Rachel," I said.

"Yes, exactly. Rachel. I didn't want to think about it. But finally I did. And I realized—but I hope I'm wrong—that the only way Alex could be really safe was if Rachel was dead, too."

Yes, of course. And Nieves didn't know all of it, perhaps. How Rachel was planning not only on sharing the money with Alex but on sharing his life, too. She loved him. She wasn't about to take no for an answer. It had to be her or Nieves.

If he went away with Nieves, if he left Rachel, she could be counted on to blow the whistle as loud and as long as she was able.

Where was Rachel now?

I made a call to her hotel. There was no answer from her room. It didn't prove anything, but I thought I knew what was happening. When Rachel had learned about Alex's death, that was her signal to meet him. At a previously arranged rendezvous, her thinking they were going to take off together.

That rendezvous was the logical place for Alex to kill her.

If only I knew where that rendezvous was.

I turned to Nieves. "Did Alex say anything about where he was going after all this?"

"No. He just told me to wait for him in Asunción. But I couldn't. I mean, robbery's one thing, but I couldn't stand it if he were really going to kill that poor woman."

I got up, trying almost physically to shake off the deadening depression that had hung over me ever since I had seen Alex.

"Come on."

"Where are we going?"

"To find Alex."

12

ALEX REANIMÉE 51

CLOVIS WAS OUR only hope. There was no one else I could think of in Paris, or anywhere else, for that matter, who might know where Alex was going to meet Rachel. Assuming Alex was still alive. And at this point I had to assume that.

I hailed a taxi and explained that we were going to make several stops. The driver complained about the loss of fares until Nieves slipped him a thousand franc note. She had a lot of class, Nieves. Of course, it also helped that she was rich.

Clovis was not at Deux Magots. We checked out the Café Flore and the Brasserie Lipp as long as we were still on the Boulevard St-Germain, but we came up empty. Next stop was the Dôme in Montparnasse. This time Nieves took charge. The manager couldn't have been more charming. He was desolated to tell her that M. Clovis had been there only half an hour ago, but had left, leaving, alas, no word as to where he might go next.

"How very annoying," Nieves said, tapping her teeth thoughtfully with a folded thousand franc note. "It is really important for me to find him this evening."

The manager's eyes shifted from the francs to the frail, from the gelt to the girl, from the moolah to the madonna, however you want to say it. Cupidity fought a brief bout with discretion and was defeated in straight falls.

"You could, I suppose," the manager said, "try M. Clovis at his home."

"And where would that be?" Nieves asked sweetly.

He was good enough to write it out for her, and she was good enough to slip him the thousand. Then we were out in the taxi again, requesting an address on the Quai d'Orsay fronting on the Seine.

Clovis lived in a big old apartment house with black wrought iron bars over the windows, and a wrought iron gate that stood like a portcullis between the street and the front door. I rang the buzzer.

Clovis himself answered the door. He was wearing an embroidered red silk dressing gown. Something that sounded nice but was unfamiliar to me was playing on the record player. I glanced at it later and saw that it was Camille St-Saëns' first symphony.

"Clovis," I said, "I'm terribly sorry to disturb you. But we come on an errand of life or death." Melodramatic, but not, I think, inaccurate.

"Well then, I suppose you must come in," he said, somewhat churlishly, I thought. But he brightened up and became the soul of graciousness itself when he took a look at Nieves.

"I hope you are going to stay in Paris for a while, mademoiselle," Clovis said. "You would be perfect for my next picture. Have you ever acted? Not that it matters. My theory on acting—"

Nieves wasn't going to get caught up in Clovis' game. "Perhaps we could discuss that some other time," she said, her smile more brilliant than ever. "Just now we have urgent business."

"Ah, yes, the famous matter of life and death. But first may I get you both a glass of wine? There is some Entrechat '84 on ice, and I also have a rather decent little—"

I wasn't going to let Clovis get into an interminable wine monologue. "Clovis, we need to find Alex at once."

He looked at me dumbstruck. "But 'Ob, you yourself saw him die!"

"I saw what I was supposed to see. But you know and I know that Alex isn't dead. You helped him set this up, didn't you?"

"I do not know what you are talking about," Clovis said frostily. "And who is this young lady?"

"She is Alex's fiancée," I told him. "The one from Paraguay. You know about her, don't you, Clovis?"

He looked at her intently. "You are Nieves?"

"Nieves de Sanchez y Issássaga," she said, her voice firm and clear, her back erect and shoulders square, like they taught her in parole-busting school. "Alex was going to meet me in Paraguay after the fake death, did you not know?"

"All right," Clovis said. "Sit down. We'll talk."

He led us into an elegant little parlor. It was filled with handblown bottles and assorted bric-a-brac, and there was a lot of stuffed furniture with gilt legs that must have cost a fortune and looked very uncomfortable.

"I recognize you by your picture," Clovis said to Nieves. "Alex showed me one of you taken in Washington. I am so pleased to meet you. Yes, Alex discussed his plan with me. I found it quite romantic. And at the same time, politically sound. I applauded Alex's skill in taking money off the evil plutocrats of Washington. And I applauded his decision to start a new life helping the poor in Africa. It was a noble gesture. I wish I could do it myself. But alas, one owes something to one's art, Rimbaud's example notwithstanding."

"Africa?" I asked. "Did you mention Africa? Just what did you think Alex was going to do there?"

Clovis smiled a sagacious smile. "He explained his dream to me in some detail. He was going to take his new identity and his money and set up a clinic in Africa. A place for the poor, the sick, the homeless. He was going to follow his role model, Dr. Albert Schweitzer. I thought it was a wonderful idea."

"Sure it is," I said. "Did he tell you where Rachel fit into all this? And Nieves?"

"But of course! That was the best part of it—the way you were all going to work together. And live together in a triune marriage. I thought that was courageous of him, thus to flaunt bourgeois morality."

"Then you know where Alex is now?" I asked.

"Perhaps, perhaps not," Clovis said, covering all the possibilities.

"This really is an emergency," I said. "Please tell us where he was going to meet Rachel."

"Ah, you know about that, do you?" Clovis said, a sly look on his foxy face. "Then you can understand the need for discretion. Do not think too badly of him, Mademoiselle Nieves, if he leaves now for Africa with Rachel and without you. The ménage à trois is inherently unstable—a part of its charm, of course, is its ephemerality."

"You have it all wrong," Nieves said. "Alex is going to marry me. Believe me, this is no delusion on my part."

"But what about Rachel, then?"

I said, "He's supposed to be meeting her somewhere and paying her off. That's what Rachel thinks. But I think Alex has other ideas."

"What are you hinting at?"

"We think," I said, "or fear, that Alex is going to kill her."

"That seems to me hardly creditable," Clovis said. But you could see him thinking. He got up and began walking around the room, running his fingers absently over the gilt furniture. Presently he turned to Nieves.

"You are sure he planned to marry you?"

Nieves nodded. "I helped make the arrangements to get him out of France."

Clovis thought about it. You could see logic wrestle with hero worship in his fevered brow. At last he asked a key question.

"Are you wealthy, Miss Nieves?"

She nodded again.

"Merde!" said Clovis. "Then it's probably true. Although I always applauded Alex's idealism, I had my doubts about it, too. The words came too easily to his tongue. Well! I have been deceived."

"Where is he?" I asked.

Clovis looked at me. His face was serious now. "What does

he plan to do when he meets Rachel, if not go away with her?"

"He's been trying to get rid of her for a long time," I said. "And now he's dead, so he can pretty much do as he pleases, and he's wealthy enough to make it come out right for him anyhow. Rachel is in the way. I can't prove any of this, but I'd like to get to Alex before Rachel does. Come on, Clovis!"

Clovis stood in the center of the room, looking like a man having an indecision fit. Then he made up his mind, turned to us, barked, "Wait, I'll be right back." And he hurried out of the room.

Nieves turned to me. "What is that supposed to mean?"

I shrugged. It was catching. The gesture, I mean.

And then Clovis came back to the parlor. He had taken off his dressing gown and put on a tough-looking leather jacket. He was wearing amber sunglasses, and he was pulling on cane-back driver's gloves.

"Come," he said, starting for the door.

"Where are we going?"

"That's a silly question," Nieves said, pulling me out the door after Clovis.

CLOVIS 52

"**Hey, look, is** it really necessary to go so fast?" I asked. The three of us were squeezed into the walnut-panelled cockpit of Clovis' restored Hispano-Suiza. An dat ole engine, she come a-whoopin' an' a-hollerin' so loud that I had to shriek over it, and got more of a note of panic into it than I intended. Clovis paid me no attention and Nieves acted like she was enjoying the whole thing. I would have enjoyed it, too, if I hadn't been so certain we were within microseconds of smearing ourselves to death against a bus or taking out a storefront with our heads.

It was late at night in Paris, past two in the morning, and traffic was thin, which was too bad because it allowed Clovis to go that much faster. I remember thinking, he's probably been waiting all his life for this, a real honest-to-God emergency, so that he can drive his stupid sports car at unsafe speeds and scare hell out of any passengers not imbued like himself with suicidal tendencies.

We barrelled up the Champs-Élysées like a jet-propelled panzer division, screamed around the Arc de Triomphe on two wheels, and then we were doing broken field running down Avenue Kléber. By some miracle we reached the Périphérique without killing anyone.

Once I heard sirens behind me. But we outran them. Be damned if we didn't outrun the radio advisories the cops were broadcasting to each other.

And then we were on the N135, going down a straight road between plane trees that turned into a blur of leafy shadows, as we eased back to a hundred miles an hour or so.

"Where are we going?" I managed to gasp.

"We're here!" Clovis shouted as he turned the car at a sign marked AÉROGARE ANNENCY.

It was a small airfield. There was steel mesh fence ahead of us and a steel mesh gate secured with a chain. Clovis didn't even slow down. He went right through it and we carried on with only one headlight to the low airport building near the airstrip.

Clovis brought the car to a skidding stop. Somewhat shakily I got out, followed by Nieves.

"What's going on here?" I asked. "Where's Alex?"

Three men came out of the darkened airport building. By the three-quarter moon I could make out that they were armed with revolvers. Jean-Claude was one of them. The second man was Nigel.

"Hi, fellows," I said, more brightly than I felt. "I don't know how you figured to come here, but I'm sure glad to see you."

"What's up with them?" Nigel asked Clovis.

Clovis was standing tall and somber in the near-darkness, tugging off his driving gloves.

"They knew," he said. "I thought it best to bring them here."

"Et tu, Clovis," I said.

Clovis shrugged. "I never promised you a rose garden."

"Hey, hey, fellows, let's lighten up," I said. "Let's all take one giant step back from the brink of this impending catastrophe, forget about Alex, go somewhere and have a couple of drinks. OK with you?"

"Get control of yourself, Hob," Nigel said sternly. "We all regret this. But you might as well go out like a man, eh?"

I stared at Nigel. He had always been a weirdo, but this was simply too much. From Jean-Claude I could expect any treachery. You get used to that from people with hyphenated first names. But Nigel? Nigel Wheaton? My old pal Nigel?

"Suppose you sit down over here while we sort this thing out," Nigel said, gesturing with the revolver.

The third man stepped into the light. Tall, light haired, smiling sheepishly. It was Alex.

And I freaked.

"To hell with this!" I cried. If I were to die in character, that meant I had to go out as a coward. I threw back my head and let out a scream that could have been heard all across France and maybe even in parts of Spain. But Clovis tapped me on the skull with a tire iron just as I was working up to full voice.

SCREAM OF THE BUTTERFLY 53

YOU COULD REALLY do a lot worse than be unconscious. You could be dead. That wouldn't be much fun, would it? So I reasoned with myself. Or rather, one part of my mind reasoned while another part floated in a luminous sea of light. I thought I could hear waves lapping against a shore, and that was strange, Paris being inland. Just as I was thinking this, I saw some figures taking shape out of the mist, and I was just getting ready to work myself into a really nice vision or hallucination or whatever you want to call it when I felt somebody shaking me. Rudely. Vehemently.

"Wake up, Hob."

It's one hell of a situation because I don't even know yet who it is who is telling me to wake up, and I know that someone's out to get me. I'm still in one of those states I get into when somebody cracks me sharply on the skull. I was sort of floaty and semi-weirded out, and my hearing was playing tricks on me. It was as though I were in a tunnel hearing scary voices which changed and distort as they bounced off the walls.

One thing was clear to me. I had misjudged this situation. Not that I held myself too much to blame for that. It's not my fault if people lie. Still, I was in trouble. On the whole, since I had no plan in mind, I thought it best to continue to feign unconsciousness. In fact, if I had only known how, I would have chosen that moment to go into hibernation. Things always look better in the spring, don't you think?

Then a familiar voice said, "Well, old boy, how are you feeling?"

I knew that voice. I opened my eyes. Alex was sitting on a low chair in front of me. He was armed with a small pistol. He wasn't exactly pointing it at me, but he wasn't exactly pointing it away from me, either.

I tried to think of something to say. The best I could come up with was, "Hi, Alex."

"Hi, old buddy," Alex said. His voice was devoid of irony. His expression was thoughtful. He was wearing chinos, and he had on a black leather flight jacket that looked really butch. He had on those reflecting sunglasses, too. That worried me. In the movies, the guys you see wearing glasses like that are about to kill somebody.

We were in a small office. I assumed it was somewhere within the airport building. Fluorescent lighting was overhead. There was light brown imitation wood panelling halfway up the walls. The ceilings were cream. There was grayish-green linoleum underfoot. There were several desks. One of them was bare, the other with a copy of *Le Monde,* a filled ashtray, a telephone. These details are of no importance, but I was hanging on to them because I was a little worried that they'd be the last things I was going to see, and when the devil asks me, "The room you were killed in, what did it look like?" I want to be able to give him a decent answer.

"You know, pal," Alex said, "you've put me into a difficult situation. Why did you have to go on investigating?"

"I guess it was because of Rachel," I said. "I couldn't let you just kill her, could I?"

"Of course you could have," Alex said. "I suppose I should have explained it to you. But I assumed you understood."

"Understood what?"

Alex rubbed his hand across his eyes and looked sadly at the ceiling. "The woman's impossible, you could see that for yourself.

She's in this life to make things miserable for as many people as possible, including herself."

"Maybe so. But that's no excuse for killing her."

"But Hob, of course it is."

"Alex, don't start up with me."

"Hob, we discussed this sort of thing many times in Ibiza. But you were a more independent thinker then. Life in America seems to have softened your head. Hob, wake up; you've been converted to television drama morality."

"Alex, I don't care what we said back then. A man talks a lot of crap in his lifetime. But you can't go around killing people because they're difficult."

"Oh, I know you can't make a habit of it," Alex said. "But an occasional one doesn't matter much, does it?"

"It's not right," I said.

"Well, of course not. But let's take it out of the abstract. A man has just one life to lead. Can you imagine leading any kind of life at all with Rachel after you?"

"Where's Rachel now?"

"She's on her way here."

"And you're going to kill her?"

Alex shook his head and shoved the gun back in his pocket. "Stop being so silly. I only kill people theoretically. I was going to buy her off."

"You think she'd let herself be bought? She loves you, Alex!"

"That's all quite true," Alex said, "and she'll be damned angry when she learns the way things really are. But I think she's a practical person. A million dollars in small bills will go a long way toward making her feel better."

"Didn't she figure to split with you?" I asked.

"Yes, but that's in the past. The real situation is, a real million in her hands in bills ought to outweigh five million in dream currency."

"Well, you know her better than I do."

"She'll come around. Don't worry about it."

Nieves came in. "I saw lights from town. Coming this way. Do you think it's her?"

"Probably," Alex said.

Nieves looked splendid. A sort of a Latin Diana Rigg. Digging the scene.

"I've been thinking," Nieves said. "Maybe I've been too softheaded about this. Do you really think she'll be trouble, Alex? Maybe you *should* kill her."

"Nieves!" I said.

She ignored me. "I mean only if you think that's best. You know more about these matters than I do."

"Hey, take it easy," Alex said. "I never planned to kill her. That was all in your mind."

"Still, it's not such a bad idea," Nieves said thoughtfully.

Clovis, Nigel, and Jean-Claude came into the room.

Clovis said, "Alex, there's something I want to ask you. All that stuff you told me about doing missionary work in Africa—you were lying to me, weren't you?"

"Not at all," Alex said. "I really believe in that. It's a part of my nature. Altruism. Ask anyone who knows me. Ask Hob; he knew me in Ibiza. But another part of my nature won't let me do that. That's the greedy part of me that's sick of being a schmuck watching other guys grab the goodies and saying, 'Tch, tch,' when the television commentators talk their usual moralistic nonsense." He turned to me. "It's the national morality play, Hob; we the people of the great t.v. audience going, 'Tch, tch,' when the commentators expose year in and year out the drama of men in authority stealing We the People blind. I figure the commentators are shrilling for the politicians because the scandal rights alone on a thing like Irangate must be worth a fortune. Well, this time I don't want to be one of the viewers; I want to be one of the takers. Get it any which way; that's the American way. I want to take the money and the girl and go to South America and live like a Mafia prince."

"But the hospital," Clovis said. "What about the hospital?"

"All in good time, old buddy, all in good time."

"But for the present, no?"

"That's right, no Africa just yet. I hear it's the hot season."

"You're going to Paraguay with this woman and live a life of luxurious capitalistic effeteness?"

"That's it, Clovis. I guess that sums it up. I guess I lied to you. But it was in a good cause."

"Self-service!" Clovis sneered.

"What better?" Alex asked.

"No," Clovis said. "I cannot permit it to end like this."

"How do you want it to end?" Alex said.

"I think you should give me a million of those dollars you stole, and I will endow a charity for African orphans."

"Actually," Nigel said, "while you're handing it out, a million for me and Jean-Claude here wouldn't go amiss."

Alex turned to me. "What do you want, Hob?"

"I'd just like to have a few of my dreams back," I said.

Alex turned to Nieves. "What do you think, darling?"

Nieves was decisive. "Give all of them half of it and let them split it up themselves. That way we all part friends and you and I still have five million left. But whatever you do, be quick about it, darling. That Paraguayan 707 with Cuch and Armadillo piloting it will be landing at any moment now."

"A 707?" Alex said. "But you knew I wanted a fighter plane."

"I wanted to accommodate you, love, but they just don't have the range. We can't refuel before Tenerife."

"You did very well," Alex said. "How did you handle the French airspace question?"

"It was not too difficult," Nieves said. "This flight is listed as a return home by an official Paraguayan observer of the recent N.A.T.O. air exercises."

We heard the sound of the plane in the distance.

Then the door burst open and Rachel rushed in.

"Hi, Rachel," Alex said. "Glad you made your connections all right. You and I have some business to attend to."

Rachel was looking at Nieves. "Who's this bimbo?"

"This is Nieves," Alex said.

"Oh, it is, is it?" She looked Nieves up and down. "Alex, are you trying to tell me what I think you're trying to tell me?"

"I'm afraid so," Alex said. "Sorry, but it just wouldn't have worked. Look, Rachel, I've got one million dollars for you." He reached into his inner jacket pocket.

"And I've got something for you, too," Rachel said, and reached into her purse and shot Alex with what sounded to me like a .38. Then she turned and put a bullet into Wheaton.

THE MEXICANS 54

I MANAGED TO knock the gun out of Rachel's hand and she turned and ran out the door. Clovis, looking shaken, followed her. Alex was standing there holding his shoulder and bleeding genteelly, nicked but not knackered. And Nigel had pulled up his shirt and found a crease along his side. The lady was not too accurate with small arms.

Just then these guys came in. There were two of them, little dark guys with bandit moustaches and big chests and guns, who looked like Mexicans and turned out to be Mexicans. It was sort of funny how they came in, drifting like an inevitable pall of smoke that has picked this place to obfuscate. I remember saying to myself, hell, another country heard from, and I noticed that Alex and Nigel and Jean-Claude were sort of drifting back toward the side door as these guys came in the front, and somehow I was in between, the only one without a gun, and it didn't look like a good place to be in.

"What I want," one of the Mexicans said, "is the sailboards. They're my property and jus' tell us where they are and there's no trouble, understood?"

"Hob has them," Alex answered immediately.

"Hey!" I said.

"Jus' a minute," the Mexican said. But Alex and the others, guns at the ready, were backing out the side door.

"Hey, jus' a minute!" the Mexican said.

"Sorry, we're late," Alex said. It was what you'd call a real Mexican showdown, but nobody opened fire and Alex, Nigel and Jean-Claude completed their exit and were gone. That left just me and the Mexicans, who didn't like the turn of events but couldn't do much about it.

To break the rather heavy silence that followed, I said, "Who *are* you guys?"

"I'm Paco," said the one who had done all the talking so far. "This is Eduardo. You mus' be Hob Draconian."

I guess I had to be, though I didn't much like it at that moment.

Paco said, "We're partners of your frien' Frankie Falcone."

"I didn't know Frankie had partners."

"Silent partners," Paco said. "We put up the money for his business. It's a lot of money, man."

"So you're partners," I said. "What are you doin' here?"

"Lookin' after our investment."

"You flew to France and are now threatening me with guns because of five sailboards?"

Paco looked annoyed. "Who gives a damn about sailboards? It's what's inside we're concerned with."

"They're made of polyurethane, aren't they?" I asked.

"Man, do I have to spell it out? We got our dope inside those boards."

I gaped at him. "Dope? You mean marijuana?"

Paco looked at Eduardo and laughed. "He thinks we're talking reefer! Are you for real? We're discussing black tar heroin, my man. The real Mexican product. The finest heroin in the world."

Suddenly it all came together for me—the black tar heroin coming into Oregon, pouring across the beaches like petroleum from a sinking ship. The savage desire of the Mexican gangs to expand their product into the lucrative café society of Europe. I later learned that it had become an obsession with them, a matter of status—to sell their heroin under the very noses of the Marseilles drug barons and win out, because French heroin is all right in its old-fashioned way but the Mexican product is new and better and above all, Mexican. It was strange, this thing of national pride. But it seemed right and natural somehow that dope dealers too, not just thieves in military uniforms, could be patriots.

"And so you see, señor," Paco went on, "it is important to us that this shipment get through. The money is of concern, of course. But we did want to enter our product in the international heroin competition being held this year at San Sebastián."

From outside I could hear the sound of an aircraft coming in for a landing. That would be Alex's ride to Paraguay. It was interesting, but it didn't matter. Right now I was faced with these guys and this was my problem.

I goggled at him. "I haven't heard about this international competition."

Paco smiled. "It is not, of course, published in the newspapers. If you didn't hear of it, señor, perhaps it is because you are not on the circuit."

As neat a snub as I've been handed in a long time. Yet I liked this man with his big automatic pistol and his guayabera shirt. I like a man who stands behind his product.

"But now, señor," he said, waving his gun with negligent purposefulness so that glints of steel danced across my eyes, and I saw, neither wisely nor too well, that I was in a world of trouble. "Now what we need most urgently from you is the location of the sailboards."

"My friend," I said, "if there were one thing I fervently wish, it would be to tell you the location of the sailboards. But alas, someone has stolen them and we are both the poorer for it."

"You won't tell?" Paco said, his voice a burlesque of menace more menacing than menace itself.

"Hombre!" I cried, ingratiating to the end, "I can't tell you because I don't know!"

Paco shook his head slowly. "Too bad," he said. "I'm afraid it's got to be the Mexican pain thing for you."

"Not the Mexican pain thing!" I cried.

"Jes, the Mexican pain thing. Eduardo! Bring the pinking scissors and the air compressor out of the trunk of the car."

"You want the edging tool, too?" Eduardo asked.

"Jes, bring the edging tool, too!"

They both smirked. It seemed that the Mexican pain thing was going to be a most comical thing to watch if you weren't the one undergoing it. So strong was my desire to be a spectator at what I was being forced to be a participant in. . . . I was in a state of confusion, and so I heard myself say, "All right, you win. We can skip the Mexican pain thing. I'll take you to the sailboards."

"You would do that, and betray your own friends?"

"Sure, as long as it's for a good cause. Like saving my own skin. That's what I'm doing, I trust?"

"Jes, you take us to the sailboards, we let you leev." His sneer belied the apparent sincerity of his words, and the twist of his lip presaged the treachery to come if we were lucky enough to even get that far.

"You have five seconds to tell us where to go," Paco said.

Great. It wasn't enough they'd given me an insolvable problem, they had to add a time limit, yet.

WHEATON 55

I DON'T KNOW how I would have stood up under torture. Luckily I didn't have to find out. Suddenly the doorway was filled with the impressive tweeded bulk of Nigel Wheaton.

"Oh, let him go," Nigel said testily. "He doesn't know anything about the sailboards."

"How do you know he doesn't know where the sailboards are?" Paco asked.

"Because I took them myself."

The Mexicans looked for a chance to do something terrible to Nigel, but he had stepped behind a filing cabinet. Besides, they had noticed that he was armed with a lightweight rapid-fire Cobra Bee Sting, the new Indonesian gun that the Israelis introduced last year at the Beirut atrocities exhibit. In his other hand he was holding a stun grenade designed to capture your attention at no greater loss than your eyesight if you happened to be caught in the wrong blink cycle when it went off.

"Sergeant," Wheaton said over his shoulder to the uniformed man whose French police cap could be dimly seen, "take these men away."

In came a sergeant followed by four uniformed French cops carrying Uzis. Another two cops broke a window and entered holding machine pistols. The Mexicans were outgunned. It was time to give up the guns and rely on the lawyers. They allowed themselves to be handcuffed and led away.

Then Fauchon entered the room, shaking raindrops out of his light blue raincoat.

"Hi, boss," Nigel said.

"Nice work, Nigel," Fauchon said.

That was my first intimation that my old buddy Nigel Wheaton was working for the police. I gave him a suitably outraged look and said, "Police informer!"

"Yes, old boy," Nigel said. "I've been working at it for some years. Ever since Inspector Fauchon helped get me out of the mess you landed me in Turkey."

I let that pass. "How did you get the sailboards?"

"Simplicity itself," Nigel said. "After our meeting in Honfleur, I didn't return to Paris. I went to the next town, St-Loup, and had a few drinks in the bar there. When Vico's flight arrived, I put in a call to him from the hotel bar. While he was diverted I hired a taxi to pick up the sailbags. Your five thousand francs came in useful for that. I put the bags into Left Luggage in St-Loup, where they presently await our pleasure."

"You might have mentioned it to me," I said.

Nigel shrugged. "And you might have gotten word to me in Turkey. Though I understand it's only natural to turn in your friends when it's the only way."

My mind brought me back, in pain, in torture, to Istanbul. The little soundproofed room in the back of the security area. Jarosik, loosening his tie and rolling up his sleeves. "No more playing around now, Hob. We know the shipment is moving. Where is it? Tell us, or take the fall yourself."

FAUCHON'S WRAP-UP 56

A GENDARME BROUGHT Rachel into the room, holding her firmly by an elbow. Fauchon's voice was not friendly when he addressed her.

"Mademoiselle," Fauchon said, "by your own admission you committed an assault with intent to kill. Only the fact that you attempted to assassinate a man whom Monsieur Draconian claimed under oath to see die several days ago prevents me from having you charged under French criminal law. I think you are not very well balanced, Miss Starr. I beg you to seek psychiatric advice when you return to your own country."

"Thanks a lot," Rachel said. She looked sort of small and pathetic. Her right arm was in a sling. She'd caught a slug back then when the bullets had been flying. "I wish to God I'd finished him, but I only winged him, and his little Latin cupcake got him out to the plane all right. You really shouldn't let embezzlers fly around in your national airspace like that."

"We don't allow it very often," Fauchon said. "In any event, it has nothing to do with me. That's the concern of a different department. Ministry of Finance, I suppose."

"To hell with all of you," Rachel said.

"Well," Fauchon said, "I suppose we have a happy ending here. As you may have guessed, 'Ob, it was the sailboard thing we were mainly interested in. We knew that such a scheme was in operation. But it was difficult to find out who was behind it. We have you to thank for that information, however indirectly." He turned to Rachel. "Did you make out all right financially? I'm just asking out of curiosity."

"It wouldn't matter if you weren't," Rachel said. "I didn't get a dime. Alex said that I had payment in full when I took that shot at him." She sighed. "I guess it was worth it at that. If only I'd pulled it another few inches to the left. . . . Well, if you don't need me any more, Inspector, I'm going on to Rome."

"You are free to leave," Fauchon said.

Rachel paused at the door. "Hob?" she asked. "Want to come along?"

I looked at her firm jaw, strong neck, righteous eyes. She was a pretty lady, but, like Alex said, she was poison. And anyhow, I had other plans.

"No, thanks," I said. "See you around."

SAILBOARDS 57

"YOU MUSTN'T THINK too poorly of Major Wheaton," Fauchon told me later. "It all happened rather quickly, the sailboards turning up like that. We weren't interested in Alex. It was the sailboards we were following all the time. When Wheaton stumbled over them in Honfleur, he knew he had to do something, not let them get away again."

"Why didn't he call a gendarme and have Vico arrested?"

Fauchon shook his head. "It was the people behind him we wanted to get. It was a brilliant move on Nigel's part to steal the boards and let the Mexicans think you were responsible."

"Were they smuggling dope in those sailboards? Is that it? I don't get it. I thought people smuggled heroin *into* the U.S., not out of it. And what was my nephew doing in that business, anyhow?"

"Some parts of the story will have to await confirmation from Falcone. But I think we will find that one of those men worked for him during the construction of the sailboards. Everyone thinks of dope smuggling in terms of big gang operations, speedboards and planes in Miami. But there's a lot more to it than that. A lot more angles. Distribution, for example, is a field worthy of study. Have you ever considered the difficulties involved in getting the dope to its end consumers, wealthy people? Especially how to do that when you need a lot of dope at a number of locations as refreshments for big-time sporting events."

"Sporting events? I've heard of athletes taking drugs, but spectators, too?"

"You better believe it, 'Ob. No one goes to a sporting contest straight any more. And these people expect to get higher when they get there." Fauchon adopted a didactic pose. I settled down for a lecture. "Dope has become a part of all sporting events. The best people use it, you know, not just the riffraff. For many, the great sports events of the year are merely excuses to gather with their friends and do a lot of dope. But where is it to come from? No one in his right mind travels with any dope on his person. No, people buy it where they are. But who are they to buy it from? Let's say you're in Monte Carlo for one of the races. You don't deal with the street gypsies. For all you know, they're police agents. Who is to vouch for them? No, you deal with someone you've dealt with before, someone you trust. You buy from one of the performers on the circuit. Like Vico."

"He's well known, Vico?"

"*Mais certainement.* He travels to all of these events, runs in all the races. And he's been dealing to his friends for years. When Vico shows up with the goods, he's going to turn over tens of thousands of dollars worth of merchandise. And this is of interest not just to himself, but to the money people behind him. And it's also the reason for the arguments between him and his brother. Enrique learned that Vico had started this questionable practice. It was Enrique who intercepted the payment. He wanted to cause Vico trouble, to try to stop him before it was too late, before either the police got him or some criminal killed him. He thought the best way would be to get your agency after Vico. Throw a scare into him. He didn't know exactly what you'd do. But your involvement would do something. And perhaps it would be enough to get Vico to stop dealing."

"But it wasn't."

"Enrique had somewhat the wrong idea. He thought Vico was able to call his shots. But he wasn't. Vico was tied in deep with his partners. They were two Mexican businessmen with criminal interests who had vacationed in Ibiza and had gotten to know Vico. The sailboards were perfect, not just for smuggling, but also for carrying the drugs around Europe. Getting the stuff in is one thing. But circulating it while it's in, that's trouble."

Fauchon was ready to go into deeper explanations. But I had heard enough. I got myself out of there. There was someone I had to see.

PÈRE LACHAISE; WAITING FOR THE SUN 58

THE LAST THING I did before plane time was go down to Père Lachaise. It's a big cemetery in eastern Paris, in the section called Belleville. I took a stroll among the illustrious dead.

There are a lot of dead here. Close to a million, the guide books say. And we got some of the biggest names in culture right here. We got Marcel Proust here and we got Edith Piaf. Modigliani's here, and so's Oscar Wilde. We got Balzac and we got Bizet; we got Colette and we got Corot. We even got Abelard and Héloïse here, and that's going back some. This is the big time. Victor Hugo said it: To be buried in Père Lachaise is like having mahogany furniture.

He's here too, of course, along with his family.

Père Lachaise is the perfect symbol for making it as a foreigner in Paris. We got Georges Ionesco, Isadora Duncan, Gertrude Stein, and Alice B. Toklas.

I nod to them, internally, of course, but they're not the ones I've come to see. The one I want lives in Block A, right over here.

Hi, Jim. Ladies and gentlemen, here lies Jim Morrison, a poet and singer of some reputation, a role model in my day, who came to Paris on a visit and is now a permanent resident.

Jim, I say, when I first came back to Paris I thought I was going to visit you and tell you what a great place you'd picked to die in, if you had to die, and how you wouldn't really mind it yourself. But then something changed and I came to say now, Jim, it's really nice here and I guess you're going to be here as long as long can be. Because they're not going to let you get out of here now. But it's wrong, Jim, you never intended to stay on here; you were just passing through. Jim, back in America there's still youth and beauty, talent and love. There's a lot of trouble, of course, but a lot of good stuff going on. I wish I could bring you back. It's a good place, America, though I'll be the first to admit that the beat, the sound of our generation, is difficult to pick up.

Why did I feel so weird? The case had worked out all right. I'd been paid.

And then I remembered that I'd forgotten to ask Jim the question.

Jim, if you were me, what would you do?

But it was too late now, I'd just have to decide for myself.

I walked back to the Place Gambetta and took a taxi out to De Gaulle. I didn't look back. I entered the airport and went to the TWA counter. It was over, my European dream. New Jersey, here I come.

It is the Paris of our dreams that entices us, we Americans in search of our past, or, if not ours, at least some past we could associate ourselves with. So that we could say, This is mine, this city, this woman, this culture, this civilization. Paris, homeland of exiles.

Alas, we don't really choose our own archetypes. They act themselves out within us. I told myself that it was better to have Paris on my mind than under my feet. Better to live in America with the memory of Paris than to live in Paris with the memory of America. The dirty old industrialized homeland calls on us to return to it precisely because it is not beautiful, not old, not hallowed. Our homeland challenges us to put our value into the place that needs it, rather than passing away our time in the place that already has it.

I had no idea what all of this meant. But in a way I did know.

Before I left, I hadn't even known there was an American civilization. And now I was returning to it.

I stood on line at the check-in counter of TWA. The man in front of me said, "Hi, buddy. You look like an American. Where you from?"

"New Jersey," I heard myself say.

"No kidding? I am, too! Whereabouts?"

"Snuff's Landing."

"No kidding! I live in Hoboken, right next door. Makes us practically kin, don't it?"

He was a jovial, nice man and I didn't want to hurt his feelings. He was wearing an electric blue leisure suit with maroon piping along the lapels, the sort of garment that haberdashers in small cities sell as leisure wear for your European holiday. Something rose up in me and snapped. "Actually," I said, "we're not kin at all. I don't really live in New Jersey. I live in Paris."

He was puzzled. "Then why are you flying to Kennedy?"

"I'm not," I said, stopping at the entrance gate. "I'm just seeing you off. Goodbye."

He gave me a funny look but he smiled and gave a little wave and then he went onto the plane. A moment later I was gone, too, back to stay with Rus and Rosemary until I could find a place of my own.

You can cash in those airline tickets any time, you know.

Before I got out of the airport I heard my name being paged. At the Hospitality Counter there was a telegram for me. It was from Harry Hamm in Ibiza. It read, INTERESTING DEVELOPMENTS. COME IMMEDIATELY.

I could see exactly how to do it. I could make a deal with Uncle Sammy through Louis and get off the hook with the I.R.S. I could turn over the New Jersey house to Mylar and good luck to her and to Sheldon, too. I'd send some money to Kate and the kids. I'd still have enough left over to set up the Alternative Detective Agency here in Paris, the world capital of pâté de foie gras, and that's not chicken liver. *Kapisch?*